SURGICAL PRECISION

A Dr. Beckett Campbell Medical Examiner Thriller

Book 3

Patrick Logan

Books by Patrick Logan

Detective Damien Drake
Book 1: Butterfly Kisses (feat. Chase Adams, Dr. Campbell)
Book 2: Cause of Death (feat. Chase Adams, Dr. Campbell)
Book 3: Download Murder (feat. Chase Adams, Dr. Campbell)
Book 4: Skeleton King (feat. Dr. Campbell)
Book 5: Human Traffic (feat. Dr. Campbell)
Book 6: Drug Lord: Part I
Book 7: Drug Lord: Part II
Book 8: Prized Fight

Chase Adams FBI Thrillers
Book 1: Frozen Stiff
Book 2: Shadow Suspect
Book 3: Drawing Dead
Book 4: Amber Alert
Book 4.5: Georgina's Story
Book 5: Dirty Money
Book 6: Devil's Den

Dr. Beckett Campbell Medical Thrillers
Book 0: Bitter End
Book 1: Organ Donor
Book 2: Injecting Faith
Book 3: Surgical Precision
Book 4: Do Not Resuscitate

This book is a work of fiction. Names, characters, places, and incidents in this book are either entirely imaginary or are used fictitiously. Any resemblance to actual people, living or dead, or of places, events, or locales is entirely coincidental.

Copyright © Patrick Logan 2019
Interior design: © Patrick Logan 2019
All rights reserved.

This book, or parts thereof, cannot be reproduced, scanned, or disseminated in any print or electronic form.

First Edition: February 2020

SURGICAL PRECISION

Prologue

"WHERE IS HE?" THE woman in the light gray suit asked as she walked briskly down the hallway. "Where's Bradley?"

The orderly beside her pointed at a thick door covered in peeling blue paint.

"Isolation," the man said flatly.

"Is that really necessary?" she asked as they continued to make their way toward the door.

"Dr. Teller, can I speak candidly?"

Claire Teller stopped in front of the door and lowered her head for a moment, before turning to face the orderly. He was in his mid-forties, solidly built, with a beard on his face and slicked black hair atop his head. But despite his appearance, his eyes were soft, and Claire knew him to be a reliable orderly, one who treated the kids with respect.

"You may."

"Okay, well, as you know, I've worked here for a long time, and I've seen a lot of kids come and go. I've seen kids come back from horrible tragedies, from all kinds of abuse. I've seen some of them become... *normal*, to go on to lead fruitful lives and become contributing members of society. I've seen others go the other way, too, and fall into a spiral of drug use and abuse. Occasionally, these kids go off the deep end—they rob, steal, even kill." As the orderly spoke, the woman turned her gaze to the window in the blue door. Sitting on the mattress in the center of the room wearing a white smock, was a young boy. He had short blond hair cut close to his scalp, and his hands were clasped on his lap.

He was staring at the wall.

"Go on," she insisted, her eyes still locked on the boy.

"Well, with Bradley... he's... he's different. I've seen a lot of kids do a lot of bad things, but nothing like him. He just snaps. He goes from like he is now—calm, compliant, even friendly—but then goes off at the drop of a hat. Loses his mind."

She finally turned to face the orderly.

"Is that it?"

The man looked at her.

"That's it."

"Then I want to thank you for being honest with me. Right now, though, I would like some time alone with him."

The orderly looked as if he were about to protest, but she held up a manicured finger, pre-emptively halting him.

"Alone."

The man sighed and pulled the key ring from his belt and unlocked the door. Then he pushed it open and allowed Claire to enter, letting her know that he was available if she needed him.

There were no chairs in the room; there was only a bucket and the mattress upon which Bradley sat. When one of the children was placed in isolation, an exceedingly rare event, every precaution was taken preventing them from having access to anything that might be used as a weapon.

Against themselves, or others.

Claire walked in front of Bradley and squatted so that they were at eye level.

"Bradley?" she said softly.

The boy looked up, his blue eyes large and wide.

Despite what the orderly had told her, it was hard to fathom that this boy could be capable of any violence at all.

But Dr. Claire Teller knew better. After working with Bradley for the better part of a year, she knew exactly what this boy was capable of.

"Bradley, what happened this afternoon?"

The boy's expression didn't falter.

"I stabbed Jimmy in the neck," he said matter-of-factly. "I stabbed him in the neck with a pencil."

Dr. Teller struggled to keep her emotions in check.

"And why did you do that, Bradley? Why did you stab him?"

The boy's reply was immediate.

"For practice."

Dr. Teller swallowed hard. She realized that her left hand had started to shake, so she tucked it behind her back and out of sight.

"Practice for what, Bradley? What are you practicing for?"

Bradley's brow suddenly furrowed and for the first time since entering the cell, Dr. Claire Teller saw unbridled hatred in the boy's eyes.

Hatred and pure evil, if such a thing existed.

"For the blond man with the tattoos," Bradley replied coldly. "That's who I'm practicing for."

PART I

Death is a Disease

Chapter 1

BECKETT THOUGHT OF RUNNING, of course, but he fought the urge. He also thought about killing, but that's what got him into this damn mess in the first place.

Instead, he simply shrugged and turned to Suzan, who had made her way up the steps to the doorway but, as per Sergeant Yasiv's orders, did not enter.

"What the hell are you looking for?" Suzan shouted into the house. Then she turned to face Beckett. "Beckett? What are they looking for?"

Another shrug.

"I've got no fucking clue."

He made his way beside his girlfriend and stared through the open door. The detective who he didn't recognize was in the kitchen now, pulling open drawers for some reason. Yasiv, on the other hand, stood at the bottom of the stairs as if debating whether or not to go up.

You're not gonna find him up there, Beckett thought. This was quickly followed by, *Maybe they won't even go downstairs. Maybe they'll just skip it, or maybe if they go into the basement, they'll somehow miss the pedophile strapped to the chair, his blood and piss soaking the plastic sheet on which he sat. Perhaps they'll even ignore the smell of the now rotting corpse.*

This final thought gave him pause.

The smell...

Trying to look natural, Beckett leaned forward a little and inhaled deeply through his nose.

His house didn't smell all that fresh, but this was nothing new; what it didn't smell like, however, was a mausoleum.

For some reason, even though he knew that the jig was up, that he was about to be found out and thrown in prison for the rest of his life, Beckett wasn't all that concerned.

If anything, he felt calmer and more relaxed than he had in a long time.

But, unfortunately, this was short-lived; a headache quickly started to build behind his eyes. In mere seconds, it felt as if someone had removed his optic nerves and was twisting them in both hands as if trying to wring water out of a towel.

"I'll check the basement," the detective suddenly hollered, clearly satisfied that Beckett's cutlery formed a complete set.

Well, Beckett thought, *there goes that idea.*

As if spurred by this comment, Suzan took a step forward, placing one foot over the threshold. Yasiv, who had since started upstairs, seemed to sense this, and he whipped around.

"Suzan, stay outside," he warned. When Suzan refused to pull her foot back, he continued, a tired look on his face, "Look, I did you guys a favor by not flooding the street with uniformed offices, but if you so much as take another step, I'll light this entire block up with blue and red lights. Is that what you want?"

During their flight, Suzan had pulled her hair up in a tight ponytail, giving Beckett a clear look at the back of her ears, which suddenly turned bright red.

You may have your ideas about what I am, Yasiv, but the last thing you want to do is to unleash the wrath of one Suzan Cuthbert.

"Suzan, I think it's probably a good idea if—"

"Oh, you did *us* a favor, did you, sergeant? Or is it detective? Maybe officer? The only favors I can see here is the one that Drake did to get you promoted. Now that's a favor. This here?" Suzan waved a finger in a tight circle. "This is no fucking favor. This is fucking harassment, that's what this is."

Something in Yasiv's face broke then, and he changed from being a stern police officer to the caring man that Beckett once knew.

The one that he'd worked with on many a case. Having been in South Carolina for the past week or so, Beckett had no idea what had changed, what evidence had led the sergeant here, to his house, and had altered the man's demeanor so drastically.

But there was no question what this was about.

It was about Wayne Cravat.

"Suzan, you should probably come over here," Beckett said in a soft voice as he watched the as of yet unnamed detective began to open the basement door.

This is it... this is the end.

"You've got nothing to say for yourself?" Suzan barked at Yasiv, who was still standing on the stairs going up.

"Suzan, I'm sorry. I am. But I've got a job to do."

"Oh, *you've got a job to do*. That's a fucking new one. Hey, Beckett, you hear that? The man has a job to do," Suzan turned to him as she spoke, but then when she saw his face, her own expression seemed to melt. "Beckett? Beckett, what's wrong?"

Beckett's eyes remained locked on the detective as he slowly disappeared into the basement.

"I think... I think you should come over here, Suzan," Beckett nearly whispered, lowering his eyes.

He figured he had thirty seconds, a minute, tops, before the detective came rushing upstairs, likely with his gun drawn, his free hand cupping his mouth in a desperate attempt to keep from vomiting on the floor. This meant that Beckett had thirty seconds to tell Suzan how he really felt about her before their relationship was permanently shattered.

"What is it?" Suzan asked, moving to his side.

Beckett's headache had fully bloomed now, which caused his eyes to water and messed with his vision. Still, he managed to reach out and wrap his arm around Suzan's small waist and pull her close.

"I love you, Suzan," he said softly in her ear. He was about to add more, to tell her how sorry he was when she suddenly pushed away.

"What the fuck, Beckett? What are they going to find down there? A secret sex dungeon?"

"I wish," he grumbled. Then he shook his head. "Seriously, there's something I need to tell you. I'm not... I'm not who..."

"You're shaking." Suzan's angry expression morphed into concern.

Beckett looked down at his hands and realized that he *was* trembling. He closed his eyes and took a deep breath, trying to will his headache and the shakes away. He managed to succeed in the latter but failed miserably in the former.

What's taking him so long? Let's just get this over with.

Beckett's basement wasn't particularly large, and Wayne was *right there*, in the middle of the room...

He took another full breath, this time exhaling slowly out his mouth.

When he opened his eyes again, Suzan was looking up at him.

She's been through so much already, what with her dad being killed, her mother taking off with her newborn stepbrother, an arrest warrant out for Drake...

But Suzan was nothing if not a strong woman, and it would take every ounce of that strength to deal with what was coming next.

"I am not who you think I am. I'm—"

"Yasiv?" the detective hollered as he re-emerged in the kitchen. "Basement's clear."

Beckett's eyes bulged, and saliva suddenly got caught in his throat. He sputtered and coughed.

Wh—wh—what? The basement's clear?

His face started to turn red as the coughing fit intensified.

It can't be clear... I left the body down there... the body of the man I murdered.

Suzan whacked him hard on the back.

"You all right?"

Beckett encouraged her to give another hard slap, and she did, finally releasing some of the phlegm from his esophagus.

"Fine," he managed to croak. "Fuck, I'm fine."

Yasiv made his way back down the stairs, a frown firmly etched on his face.

"Upstairs appears clear, too," the sergeant said, his disappointment palpable.

Oblivious to what was going on inside the house, Suzan turned to him.

"Beckett? What were you gonna say?"

Beckett swallowed again, making sure that the saliva made it all the way down into the pit of his stomach before replying this time.

"I was gonna say, that these goons have no right to judge me. So what if I like to wear lady's underwear in my own time? I have beautiful thighs, and it's no crime to want to show them off. Yasiv, if there's anything missing from my underwear drawer…"

Chapter 2

SERGEANT YASIV AND HIS MINION spent another thirty minutes going over the place, but it was obvious that this was just for show. They'd expected to find a body and hadn't come prepared to search with a fine-toothed comb.

Beckett, sitting on the stoop with his arms wrapped around Suzan, was caught in a constant loop of confusion and disbelief.

He had no idea what happened to Wayne Cravat's corpse but figured that there were only three possible explanations: one, the man had somehow recovered from his injuries and left on his own accord; two, Beckett had moved the body and forgot about it; three, he had never killed the man in the first place.

Yeah, Beckett, that makes sense. Wayne managed to stem the bleeding from his carotid artery and just walked away. Out of courtesy to his would-be murder, he cleaned up the mess on the way out. Or maybe you were sleep walking and decided to move a two-hundred-and-fifty-pound man to... where? A neighbor's house? The mall? Or perhaps you just imagined the sensation of warm blood spilling on your hands as you drove the scalpel into the man's fat neck and then conjured up the acrid smell of urine...

"What the hell is this all about, anyway?" Suzan demanded when Sergeant Yasiv finally made his way to the front door.

Yasiv's face contorted.

"I can't discuss an ongoing investigation."

"To hell, you can't; you better tell us what the fuck is going on here, Sergeant. Beckett is a respected pathologist, a senior medical examiner for the goddamn state of New York. If you don't tell us, I'll go to the press. I'll tell them all about this harassment, about—"

Beckett put a comforting hand on Suzan's shoulder, trying to ease the tension in her muscles. Then he brought her close.

"Just let it go."

Suzan looked up at him.

"Let it go? Why would we *let it go*? These assholes can't just invade our privacy like this, embarrass us in front of all the neighbors."

Beckett looked around quickly and noted that there were no neighbors out, at least none that he could see. But he exercised his better judgment and resisted the urge to mention this to Suzan. Besides, even if someone did see the two detectives, there were plenty of reasons why they might show up at the Senior Medical Examiner's house, none of which included searching for Wayne Cravat's body.

The body that he somehow managed to misplace.

Did I... did I just imagine everything that happened with Wayne? The video? The well-planned, if moderately clichéd, speech?

Beckett shook his head. That was ridiculous. He had a tattoo on his ribs as a permanent reminder of what he'd done to the sick pervert.

"Suze, I think it's best if we just let it go, given my... past." He stared at Suzan as he said this, focusing in on her bright blue eyes.

My past, which includes killing serial killer Craig Sloan... in self-defense, of course.

The single most important act in his life, the one that had set him on this path.

"I don't know how you did it, Beckett," Yasiv said as he stepped onto the stoop. "I don't know where—"

Beckett suddenly reached out with his right index finger and flapped it against Yasiv's still moving lips. The sergeant was so surprised by this, that it took him nearly a full second before he swatted Beckett's hand away.

"What the fuck do you think you're doing?"

Beckett stepped back and then brought his finger, which was moist with Yasiv's saliva, to his nose and sniffed it dramatically.

"That's weird," he said, to no one in particular.

"Don't ever touch me," Yasiv warned.

Beckett ignored him and held his finger up for Suzan, Yasiv, and the other detective to see.

"The strange thing is, even though you're talking all kinds of bullshit, your breath doesn't even stink."

Yasiv scowled and looked for a moment as if he were about to lash out at Beckett, which would've made the latter extremely happy, but instead, he just reached into his pocket and pulled out a cigarette.

Without another word, Yasiv gestured at the detective, and together they made their way down the driveway to their car.

"Bye-bye now, Yasiv. So nice to see you," Beckett hollered after them. "Come back and visit anytime!"

The sergeant opened the car door and was about to slide inside, before pausing and looking back at Beckett.

"You think this is funny? You think this is fucking funny, Beckett? I won't stop. I won't—"

"Just get in the car, Yasiv," the detective suggested.

Yasiv looked over at his partner, took a huge drag of his smoke, then did just that.

"Yeah, listen to your mommy and get the fuck out of here," Beckett shouted, no longer caring if the neighbors overheard. "It's time for dinner."

The unmarked police car took off like a shot. When it was out of sight, Beckett took a deep breath, and then picked up the bags and turned to Suzan, offering her a wan smile.

"Well? Should we get unpacked? Because hell, I'm hungry. How 'bout you? Could you eat? I'm craving those chicken and waffles we had down south."

Chapter 3

"You're seriously gonna make a sandwich right now?" Suzan asked, hands on her hips.

Beckett shrugged as he slid two slices of bread into the toaster.

"It's either that or unpack the bags, and I don't want anything to do with laundry right now. Besides, I'm hungry."

While on the outside, Beckett was doing his best to appear calm and collected, his eyes kept drifting to the partially opened basement door.

Where the fuck are you, Wayne?

"Beckett, can't you just be serious for once? What the hell was Yasiv doing here? What the hell were they looking for?"

Beckett turned his back to Suzan and started to rifle through the refrigerator.

"We don't have any of that extra fatty, double gluten, hyper-GMO, heavily-processed pork-like product left? Damn."

He was about to close the fridge when he spotted an anemic slice of black forest ham tucked near the back. He pulled it out, took one whiff, and then recoiled violently.

"Yikes," Beckett said as he tossed it in the garbage. Reaching back into the fridge, he found a block of cheese that hadn't yet eclipsed its Best By date.

"Don't change the subject, Beckett. I know enough about cops, about how they work, from my dad. I know that they don't just give out search warrants. They needed a reason to come here. I'm getting pretty fed up with all these damn secrets."

Beckett turned around then, clutching the block of cheese in his hand. He looked at Suzan and raised an eyebrow, trying desperately to read her mind.

What are you really asking, Suze?

"And don't even think of telling me you have a headache, either," Suzan remarked. "Dr. Blankenship gave you a clean bill of health, remember?"

I do have a headache, Beckett thought. But he knew better than to say this.

"Fine, okay, they were here because—" the toast popped, and Beckett threw up his hands as if to say, *Oops sorry, got interrupted.* He turned around, retrieved the toast, and jammed the entire block of cheese between the two slices. It was the strangest sandwich he'd ever made, but it served its purpose: it gave him a few more seconds to come up with a lie that Suzan wouldn't see right through.

"Look, I don't want you to get involved in this, Suzan, but if you *must* know, it has to do with this case... this case about a dead woman's husband. The police and the DA thought that the woman had killed him, as did one of the other Medical Examiners. But I wasn't so sure. And you know how I am, all noble and shit. I took a look at the body and came up with a different explanation. Fucked up their whole case, and they're none too happy about it."

Wow, Beckett thought. *That was pretty good. And true... the story, that is; not the context.*

He took a bite of the sandwich, then grimaced. It was so dry that he couldn't even hope to swallow it.

"Delicious," he croaked, bits of dried bread spraying from his lips. He held it out to Suzan. "You want some?"

Suzan scowled and shook her head.

"That's fucked up," she remarked, reaching for the search warrant that Beckett had haphazardly thrown on the counter. As she started to read, Beckett got onto his tippy toes, realizing that he hadn't even looked at the damn thing.

He doubted, however, that it would say anything about Armand or Greta Armatridge, or about the fact that an owl had actually killed her husband.

A goddamn owl...

Suzan deliberately tilted the page away from him. There was nothing Beckett could do but choke down another mouthful of the terrible sandwich while he waited.

Eventually, Suzan tossed the single sheet of paper back onto the counter.

"Doesn't say anything."

Beckett shrugged.

"It'll blow over," he offered. "They're just pissed because I went against the grain. It'll pass."

I hope, Beckett thought. *I really hope this shit blows over.*

He thought back to all the people he'd killed, starting with Craig Sloan, and ending with Reverend Cameron and his wife. Not all had been clean, and some had even been sloppy, most notably Bob Bumacher. That had been messy. What made it worse was that was the case that Karen Nordmeyer had signed off on it at his behest. The same Medical Examiner whom he'd contradicted in the Armatridge report.

Karen Nordmeyer... she was so pissed when I —

Beckett's eyes suddenly narrowed.

Fucking hell, I bet she was the one who went to Yasiv, that brown-nosing, mousey little cunt. She probably told him about Bob.

"Beckett, you okay?"

Beckett opened his mouth to speak, but a bolus of toast mixed with processed cheese had lodged itself in his windpipe.

Fuck!

He pounded on his chest trying to clear the blockage, but it was stuck good.

Great, he thought. *After all the people I've killed, after everything I've gotten away with, all the drugs I've done, including the cocaine on Donnie DiMarco's yacht, this is how I go out? Choking on the worst fucking sandwich in human history?*

He tried to force the food down by blinking hard like a frog, but that proved futile.

Goodbye, sweet world. It's been a slice.

Something struck him hard between the shoulder blades and the piece of food dislodged from his throat. It landed on the counter and stuck there with a sickening 'plop'.

Beckett dropped the remainder of the sandwich, then put both hands on the edge of the counter and sucked in a huge breath.

"Jesus, Beckett," Suzan said from behind them. "Eat much?"

After catching his breath, Beckett turned to look at Suzan. She was staring at him, wide-eyed.

"You okay?" he asked, wincing at the rawness in his throat.

Suzan blinked.

"Am *I* okay? Are *you* okay?"

Beckett dropped his eyes to the disgusting hunk of food on the counter, then the even more unappealing sandwich and shook his head.

"No, not really. I could use something to drink… a beer, maybe."

Suzan rolled her eyes.

"Let me guess, they're in the basement."

Beckett nodded.

"Fine, I'll get you one, but only because you nearly died."

With that, Suzan turned and started toward the basement door.

"Thanks, honey bunch," Beckett said. Suzan had taken the first step downstairs when he realized his mistake. "Wait, I'll get it! You sit down, put your feet up, run a bubble bath or something. I'll get it! *I'll get it!*"

But it was too late; Suzan had already disappeared into the darkness.

Chapter 4

"ONLY TWO LEFT," SUZAN proclaimed as she emerged from the basement, a beer in each hand.

Beckett exhaled audibly.

What the hell is going on here?

"You sure? I'm positive there was a whole case down there before we left for South Carolina."

Suzan shrugged and handed him a beer. Beckett popped the top, slipped the cap in his pocket, and took a sip.

It tasted real. Nothing else about what had happened since coming home seemed real, but the beer was.

As was his headache.

Alcohol probably wasn't the best cure, but it was a fantastic numbing agent.

"I only saw two."

"I'll take a look," Beckett offered. Before Suzan could protest, he slid by her and headed down to the basement.

The first thing that hit him was the smell; or, more precisely, the lack thereof.

In his mind, this meant that either the place had been recently fumigated — unlikely — or whoever was responsible for removing Wayne Cravat's body, had done it while it was still fresh.

The second thing that Beckett noticed was that there was no body.

There was no body, there was no plastic sheet, there was no chair, there was no piss, there was no blood. Even the projector upon which he'd played the video of Wayne finding Bentley Thomas's corpse was missing.

"What the hell," he muttered.

"Relax, we've got a bottle of wine and some scotch if you really want to tie one off tonight," Suzan hollered from upstairs. "But remember, you've got work tomorrow."

Work? The only work I expected to do after Yasiv arrived was making license plates in the pen.

Beckett stood with his hands on his hips for a moment and looked around.

He was losing his mind. This was his basement, and it was just the way he remembered it.

Except there was no body. He'd killed Wayne Cravat right here, right in this very room with —

"And you're out of food, too," Suzan shouted. "You feel like pizza or Chinese?"

"What I feel like, is finding out what the hell happened to the man I killed down here," Beckett whispered.

"What's that?"

"Nothing, dear."

He was about to shut off the lights and head upstairs, intending on dealing with this later when he had less of a headache and more of a clear frame of mind, when he spotted something on the concrete floor.

Squinting hard, Beckett walked over to the stain and got on his knees. It was only a mere speck, the size of a dime, maybe even smaller, and in their hurry, he wasn't surprised that Sergeant Yasiv and his boyfriend had overlooked it.

Evidently, they were searching for something larger, like a two-hundred-and-fifty-pound man with his throat slit.

Beckett placed his thumb on the stain and then held it up to the light. When he rubbed the coppery brown powder between thumb and forefinger, there was no questioning what it was.

Blood.

He knew that he should be relieved that he wasn't actually losing his mind, that he had killed Wayne Cravat in this room after all.

But he wasn't.

If anything, Beckett was even more frightened.

Because someone had cleaned up his mess.

Someone knew his secret.

And that was utterly terrifying.

Chapter 5

BECKETT STARED AT THE ceiling until the shapes started to morph into faces of people he knew.

Faces of the people he'd killed.

He blinked and then looked over at Suzan who was snoring softly at his side. She was lying on her chest with her arms up beneath the pillow.

He stared at her for a while, not just because she was more pleasant to look at than the faces of the people he'd murdered, but because she was... well, attractive.

Beautiful, even.

His headache had thankfully subsided—paradoxically, a beer and a fist of scotch had helped make it go away. But what hadn't died down, was the impending feeling of doom.

Someone had tipped Sergeant Yasiv off, and, more importantly, someone had removed Wayne Cravat's corpse from his basement.

Where they had taken the body was another story altogether.

But the *why*... Beckett had seen enough blackmail movies to know that whoever it was hadn't done him a solid and just incinerated Wayne. No, the body was somewhere safe, somewhere hidden and discrete, yet also available in case they needed to bring it out again.

Should Beckett not do what they wanted.

But how the fuck am I supposed to know what they want?

With a sigh, Beckett threw the sheet back and rose to his feet. Then he looked down at himself, at the tattoos on his chest and on his arms. As he made his way over to the window and pulled the curtain back to illuminate the room with the bluish glow of moonlight, he lifted his right arm and stared at the horizontal stripes beneath.

He had two more to add; one for Alister and one for his wife.

Thinking back now, though, Beckett was starting to regret his decision to head to South Carolina in the first place. He'd tried to be clean and neat, to stay in the shadows, but that had all gone out the window when he'd met Reverend Cameron. Instead, Beckett had made quite a scene at the church.

If anybody was watching me there, and then broke into my house...

Beckett shook his head. What was in the past had to stay there. He had to look forward. He had to keep his head down, steer clear of any situation that might expose him, and just wait for this to blow over.

But dead bodies barely blow over—you should know this, Beckett; you are, after all, New York State's Head Medical Examiner.

Beckett was about to close the curtain when his eyes fell on a black Lincoln Town car parked across the street that he'd never seen before. Normally, this wouldn't set off alarm bells, it was New York City, but his suspicions were heightened. He tried to glimpse into the car, but the windows appeared tinted and with the moonlight reflecting off them, it was impossible to see anything at all.

"What are you doing?" A soft voice from the bed asked.

Beckett let the curtain fall back into place.

"Nothing. Can't sleep."

Suzan was still lying on her stomach, her bare breasts pushed in the mattress. She looked exactly the way she had moments ago when he'd stepped out of bed, only now her eyes were open.

"Thinking about the body?"

Beckett's skin suddenly broke out in goose pimples.

"The body?" he nearly gasped.

Suzan yawned, and her eyes slowly closed.

"Yeah, the body you told me about..."

Beckett could hardly believe what he was hearing.

I told her about the body? While I was asleep? What did I say? What the hell did I say?

As Suzan's breathing started to regulate and he feared that she was drifting off to sleep, Beckett strode across the bedroom, and gently placed a hand on her shoulder. Her eyes opened halfway.

"What body, Suzan?"

Suzan smiled, her perfect lips parting just a little.

"The body... Armando or whatever... you know, the report that you changed the cause of death? The reason why the police are hounding you?"

Beckett breathed a sigh of relief.

"Yeah, *that* body. Thinking about it, sure. Get some sleep."

Suzan's smile turned into a small frown.

"You need your sleep, too," she remarked. "You have to work tomorrow."

"Which means you have to work, too," Beckett said as he slid beneath the covers.

He put his hands over his chest and stared at the ceiling again, but when the faces of his victims started to appear, he shut his eyes.

At some point, Beckett must've fallen asleep because the next thing he registered, was his alarm clock blaring in his ear like a rooster with strep throat.

Chapter 6

OF COURSE, EVEN THOUGH Beckett had been practically awake when his alarm went off, he was still racing to get out of the house on time.

"Aren't you gonna eat something?" Suzan asked as he threw on his best shirt—an L.L. Bean polo that was wrinkled at the bottom.

"No, I'm all right. Intermittent fasting and all that," he said as he slapped his stomach. They were both well aware that he'd lost weight over the past month or so, and that his body was slowly transitioning from an athletic build to just plain skinny.

And, as a doctor, Beckett knew that the next phase on the continuum was skinny fat. There was nothing worse than skinny fat. It was like being agnostic. Just make up your fucking mind already.

He leaned over and kissed Suzan on the cheek.

"You all right? Sleep well?" she asked.

Beckett wondered if she recalled their conversation but decided not to inquire about it.

"Like a baby who just suckled on a teat. Speaking of which, don't forget that you've got anatomy class in an hour or so. Just because you're sleeping with the prof, doesn't mean you can skip it."

Suzan rolled her eyes.

"Yeah, right. We both know that you're going to be the one to skip class... and leave me to teach it."

"Ah, the perennial perks of bedding the TA."

***

"What the fuck," Beckett said as he pulled into the NYU Medical parking lot.

The black Lincoln Town Car was back. He'd noticed it within five minutes of leaving his house but had dismissed the idea that he was being followed.

He didn't want to add paranoid to his growing list of pathologies.

But now, as the car rolled past the parking lot, moving at a pace that suggested the occupants wanted Beckett to know that it was there, his suspicion had become impossible to ignore.

"Yasiv, you prick," he grumbled as he slammed his car into park and then sprinted out onto the road.

But the Lincoln was gone.

The last thing Beckett wanted right now was a tail, but it wasn't as if he could lodge a formal complaint against Yasiv; that would only focus the spotlight on him.

Just lay low. This will blow over.

Beckett ran a hand through his bleach-blond hair.

"Lay low... since when have I ever laid low?"

Still scowling, Beckett made his way through the halls of the University until he came to the Pathology Department.

He had some time to kill before meeting his residents and had already decided to put out a few feelers to see if a body had mysteriously shown up. But first, he needed a coffee. The good news was that after hooking the secretary Delores up with Chris Hemsworth, the woman had taken it upon herself to get him a coffee each and every morning.

Except it appeared that the string of surprises that had started with Sergeant Yasiv's visit weren't over yet.

Delores wasn't behind her desk.

In her place was a thin black girl with spiky curly hair.

"Who are you?" Beckett asked.

The woman pressed her lips together.

"Who are *you*?" she shot back.

Beckett made a face; he wasn't in the mood for this.

"Your boss. Where's Delores?"

He expected an apology, but none came.

"Family emergency. I'm a temp; the name's Latasha."

"Medical?"

"Excuse me?"

Beckett sighed.

"Delores's family emergency... is it medical?"

"I got no idea. I'm just a temp."

"Ain't that the truth," he grumbled as he made his way to his office.

Beckett put his key in the lock and turned it. But when it came to opening the door, he took his time. Ever since the organ deliveries a while back, he'd been cautious. And now, given what had transpired since, he wouldn't be completely surprised to find some mail waiting. A ransom note, perhaps.

But despite being gone for nearly a week, his desk was surprisingly devoid of mail.

People were still taking a wide berth around him after the Craig Sloan incident. This was only exacerbated by the fact that Beckett didn't fit in, that he didn't golf or wear bespoke suits or jerk off the mayor. It was almost as if they'd been looking for a reason to alienate him ever since he became one of the youngest Senior MEs in New York State history.

Well, now they had plenty of reasons.

But while they could, and had, stifled his Medical Examiner case load, they couldn't stop him from teaching his classes.

They couldn't stop him, because Beckett had the only thing that was more ironclad than death and taxes: he had tenure.

Which meant that he could pretty much do whatever he wanted and still keep his University position. And there's nothing that would make Beckett feel better on this already shitty morning then being able to torture his residents, if only for an hour or two.

Chapter 7

"WHY ARE YOUR BLINDFOLDS off?"

When none of the medical residents said anything—they just looked at each other—Beckett repeated the query.

"I told you not to take them off until I got back." When still nobody replied, Beckett aimed a finger directly at one of the residents. "Pedro? I need an answer."

The man shifted uncomfortably in his chair, then looked to his neighbor before finally speaking up.

"You've been gone a week, Dr. Campbell. I—*we* didn't think you were serious about keeping them on. That's... that's ridiculous."

Beckett was amazed that no matter how many times he fucked with his students, they continued to fall prey to his pranks. Mommy and Daddy told them not to question authority, to just bow their heads, knuckle up, and do as they were told. He'd once heard that if you took someone out of the early twentieth century and plunked them into today, there were only two institutions they would recognize: schools and hospitals.

Hospitals were obvious; they were full of dead and dying people today, in the past, for always. But schools? A relic of the industrial era, schools were designed to prepare people for munition production during wartime. Shit, even the use of a bell was intended to get students conditioned to an aural assault meant to signify a shift change.

And yet this archaic model persisted today, in pretty much the exact same form as a hundred years ago.

Even his students, supposedly some of the brightest pathology residents in the country, all future leaders of the medical community, appeared stuck in this mold.

Which means I'm failing, Beckett thought. *I need to push them harder. Take them out of these sterile walls. Show them the real world.*

He felt like a momma bird pushing her beloved hatchlings off the highest branch.

Fly, my pretties; fly.

"Right then. Looks like we're gonna have to go on a field trip."

Eyebrows were raised, but no one dared speak up.

"Well? Aren't you gonna ask where we're going?"

"What about the chapters you told us to read? Aren't you going to test us on them?"

Beckett looked at the man who'd spoken. It was Grant McEwing, of course; Boy Wonder, Doogie Houser, Ted Bundy. Brother to Flo-Ann McEwing, who had taken up permanent residence as a tattoo beneath Beckett's right arm.

And of course, he wanted a test; Grant had an eidetic memory. But that wouldn't help him on this trip.

A smirk appeared on Beckett's lips. When he'd suggested a field trip, it had felt right, but he hadn't known where he was actually going to take them.

But now… now Beckett knew exactly where they were going.

"Oh, we can have a test all right, but this won't be like any you've taken before. Have you guys seen Fear Factor?"

More confused looks and Beckett's smile grew.

"Ah, I'm dating myself. Anyways, it's probably better that you don't know."

With that, Beckett rose and slipped his bag over one shoulder. He knew that Suzan would be pissed that he was taking off again, especially considering the fact that she was indeed going to teach the anatomy class after all, but he needed some space.

Beckett was nearly to the door before he realized that no on had risen out of their seats to follow.

"C'mon," he said, turning back. "Of everything I've done, you think this is a joke? Get your bags, we're going on a road trip."

At long last, the residents started to rise, but they weren't moving quick enough for Beckett's liking. It would take almost an hour to get to their destination and he had other things to do today.

Like find Wayne Cravat's corpse.

"Chop, chop, people," he said, clapping his hands together. "They're not gonna wait forever."

It was a strange thing to say, and Beckett tilted his head to one side.

"Well, yes, I guess they will be there forever. Forever and a day, as the saying goes."

"Uh, Dr. Campbell?" Maria asked.

"Yeah?"

"Are you all right?"

Beckett chuckled.

"Never better."

"And are you going to tell us where we're going?"

"The meat factory, dumb-dumb," Beckett said as he stepped into the hallway. "That's what I call it, anyway. Them sophisticated types refer to it as a Body Farm. Personally, I think it's a bit of a misnomer. A farm is a place where plants go from seedling to beautiful flower. In a Body Farm, all the nice things just turn into rot and decay."

Chapter 8

BECKETT DIDN'T LIKE TO play favorites—like religion, he loathed every resident equally—but in the end, he agreed to allow Grant McEwing to join him in his car.

After all, he had murdered the man's sister.

The first thirty minutes or so were relatively quiet, for which Beckett was grateful. Even though he tried his best to bring Grant out of his shell, to make him less socially awkward, the man was resistant.

Beckett didn't really blame him, though; after all, he had never even graduated Medical School—he had just forged his documents with help from the late Dr. Ron Stransky. And if anybody knew about secrets, it was Beckett.

Still, this silence eventually became annoying and then frustrating, as Beckett's thoughts circled back to Wayne Cravat.

And Yasiv.

His headache.

His tingling fingers.

His tattoos.

The fact that he was missing a fucking body.

"Hey, I just wanted thank you for helping me out by running the genetic tests on those samples I sent you," he said at last.

"No problem," Grant replied.

Beckett waited for the man to say more, but he fell silent after just those two words.

Jesus, it's like pulling teeth with this guy.

"Your curiosity knows no bounds," Beckett joked.

Still nothing.

"Don't you want to know why I asked for those tests? I mean, a good pathologist is always asking questions, trying to—"

"I know why you wanted those tests."

Beckett was surprised by the reply and tried his best not to let it show on his face.

"Right, and why is that? Humor me."

"Because of that Reverend, the one who said he can cure death. I remember seeing the article on your desk a while back."

That fucking memory...

"Go on..."

"Well, when you sent me the samples with postage from South Carolina, I figured that's where you were. It was pretty easy to put together the specific genetic tests you wanted and the supposed diseases that the Reverend was curing."

Curious now as to how much the man knew about Alister Cameron and his claims, Beckett asked Grant directly.

"The Reverend and his wife? Well, he is being accused of trapping sick people in his basement, using them as props to convince others he could cure the incurable. After they were found out, they fled. The cops are being pretty mum about it, saying that they are only persons of interest, but I suspect that more information will come out soon."

Beckett swallowed hard.

"Why do you think more—" he cleared his throat, which had suddenly started to itch. "Why do you think more information will come out soon?"

"Heard some rumblings on Reddit, might be a Podcast or two about the Reverend and his wife in the works. A Sword and Scale episode, or maybe Casefile. They do some good in-depth investigations of these types of cases."

Oh, great, Beckett thought. *That's all I need. Some geeked up Internet reporter digging into what actually happened in South Carolina.*

He thought back to the episode when Alister Cameron had touched his forehead and he'd pretended to speak in tongues. So far as he knew, nobody had been recording the service, but if they were, and that video was to surface...

If all Yasiv was working on now were the words of a disgruntled fellow employee by the name of Dr. Karen Nordmeyer, how deep would he dig if he could link Beckett to Alister and Holly's disappearances?

Balls deep, that's how deep.

Beckett suddenly considered the possibility that it was Grant who moved Wayne's body. After all, the man had a motive and he was incredibly intuitive, if socially inept.

This line of thinking pushed Beckett even deeper down the rabbit hole.

What about Screech? Could he have moved the body?

He had been there on the yacht, and even though the man had never said anything about Donnie DiMarco or Bob Bumacher, there was an understanding when he looked at Beckett.

If anybody knew anything about Beckett's dark secret, it was Screech.

But why?

Sure, their relationship had been strained of late, but Beckett had done numerous favors for the man, including re-opening the Armatridge case.

"Dr. Campbell, can I ask you something?"

It could also be Dr. Nordmeyer herself. She could have moved the body, put it somewhere with the intention of blackmailing him later. The woman had made no secret of the fact she had aspirations of becoming a Senior Medical Examiner.

No, not *a; the* Senior Medical Examiner.

The position that Beckett presently held.

The stoplight ahead of them turned red, and Beckett slowed. It was then that he noticed the black Lincoln crawling through the intersection in the opposite direction.

"You motherfucker," he grumbled. He debated gunning the red light, but the driver of the Lincoln must have considered this option as well because he suddenly sped up.

"Excuse me?" Grant said.

"No, not you."

The light turned green and Beckett crept forward, craning his neck all the way around to see if he could catch a glimpse of the license plate as the car disappeared out of view. He couldn't.

That asshole Yasiv is tailing me; I'm sure of it now, he thought.

"Dr. Campbell?"

Beckett noticed a discrete sign for the Body Farm and pulled into the parking lot that was practically invisible from the road.

"No, not now," he said flatly. "Ask me later. Right now, we're going to see some bodies."

Chapter 9

"SO, THESE ARE THE new residents, am I right?" the man with the thick black beard asked as he strode forward, hand outstretched.

"That's what the Uni tells me," Beckett replied with a grin. He grabbed the man's hand and shook it briskly. "Dr. Swansea, it's been a while."

"Too long," Swansea said with a similar grin of his own.

The man's beard made up for the lack of hair on the top of his head, but unlike those who tried to comb or brush it in every which way to cover up the bald spot, Dr. Swansea had gone for the clean-shaven look. And it suited him.

The man had dark eyes that matched his beard, eyes that were flanked by more creases than Beckett remembered.

He supposed, however, that he didn't look like a spring chicken, either.

"This is Dr. Swansea," Beckett said, turning to the students behind him. "He runs the show here at the Body Farm and is one of the best forensic pathologists I've ever met."

"Oh, stop, you're making me blush," Dr. Swansea said. "Care to tell me their names?"

Beckett hesitated, and the man chuckled and slapped him on the back.

"Of course, you've got the memory of a goldfish. I'm surprised that you even passed your medical boards—or maybe you didn't? Maybe you just bribed somebody. After all, you don't look like any doctor I've ever seen."

Before Beckett could say anything, the man stepped in front of him and introduced himself.

"What's with all these formalities? You getting soft on me, Swansea?" Beckett offered as he wrapped his arm around the man's shoulder and together, they started towards the small, brown building.

"You're the one who's tied down if the rumors are true. Anyways, I'm glad you came by. As you said, it's been too long."

The New York State Body Farm was one of the most impressive units that Beckett had ever done a rotation in. In fact, in the three months that he'd spent at the Body Farm, he gained more insight into death, and therefore life, than perhaps the rest of his residency combined.

Spread over nearly six acres, the Body Farm was home to more than five hundred cadavers, all kindly donated by the recently departed.

After a brief presentation by Dr. Swansea, in which he outlined some of the basic goals of the Body Farm, it was time for the real fun.

The tour.

But when the doctor took one look at the sneakers that the residents were wearing, he frowned.

"It's pretty wet out there."

It was Trever or Taylor or Tyler or whatever the hell his name was who spoke up.

"These are all I got."

"Let me guess, your benevolent leader didn't tell you where you were going."

Beckett held up his hands.

"To be honest, I didn't know either. I just went for a drive and stumbled upon this place. Who would've thunk it?"

Dr. Swansea shook his head.

"Not a problem. We just got a shipment of used boots in plenty of sizes."

As the residents started to gear up, donning white plastic suits and well-worn boots, Dr. Swansea came up to Beckett.

"How you doing, man?" he asked in a low voice. At first, Beckett wasn't sure what Dr. Swansea meant, but then he realized that he'd probably heard about the incident with Craig Sloan and his so-called 'vacation'.

Beckett shrugged.

"Meh, the medical community treats me like a leper, but then again, that's nothing new."

Dr. Swansea nodded.

"Well, you know we always have room for more doctors out here if you get sick of the city."

This wasn't the first time that the man had extended such an offer, but it was the first time that Beckett thought he really meant it.

"Thanks, but I'll tough it out. I don't mind the city and I'd miss the University too much. Good pay and tenure and all that."

Dr. Swansea observed him for a second longer than was comfortable, then gave his shoulder an encouraging squeeze.

"All right, this isn't a fashion show," the doctor said, turning back to the residents. "Pick a pair of boots and let's get going. I've got this spectacular beehive I want to show you."

Chapter 10

NO STRANGER TO DEATH, Beckett was nonetheless taken aback by the scene before him.

The male corpse was hanging from a branch by a soiled stretch of rope. His face was a deep shade of purple, and it was so malformed that it was hard to make out any specific features. From the neck down, things just got worse. He'd been sliced from sternum to pubis, and the left half of his rib cage had been broken open and pulled wide. The cavity, devoid of organs, was now filled with honeycomb.

Hundreds, perhaps thousands, of bees moved in and out of the man's corpse.

"Wow," was all Beckett could say. Most of the residents were standing directly behind him, but Maria was standing a good twenty feet back. Under most circumstances, he might've scolded or teased her, but in this case, he gave her a pass.

Beckett let his eyes drift down the corpse, all the way to the feet, which were massively swollen.

"All right, I'll bite. Why in the fuck would you put a hive of bees in this poor guy's chest?"

Dr. Swansea chuckled.

"Well, as much as this seems like it's just a fun after school art project, there's a rhyme and reason to it. Anybody care to tell me what's different about this scene? Besides the obvious, of course."

Beckett squinted at the corpse, and then it struck him. He was about to blurt out the answer when Dr. Swansea shook his head.

"Not you, Beckett. One of the kids."

A bee landed on Beckett's lip and he swatted it away.

"Come on, don't embarrass me in front of Dr. Swansea. If you don't know the answer, ask him some damn questions."

Grant immediately spoke up.

"How long has the body been hanging here?"

"Five days."

"And he was placed there fresh? Out in the open, just like this?" Grant continued.

Dr. Swansea smiled, and Beckett found himself doing the same. He knew where this line of questioning was headed.

"He was—hung as soon as we got the body. Like Wendy's hamburgers, he was never frozen."

That was it. That was the comment that sent Maria over the edge.

She buckled over and vomited, and then shook violently. Beckett quickly went to her and draped an arm over her back.

"All right, it's all right," he said softly. Pedro appeared and started to rub her back.

"Looks like you might be the one who's getting soft, Beckett," he heard Dr. Swansea say with a chuckle.

Beckett ignored the comment and looked over at the other residents. Taylor had a bottle of water with him, and he signaled for the man to bring it over. He handed it to Maria who swished the liquid around in her mouth for a moment and then spat.

"I'll be okay," she said, rising to her full height.

She lied.

Almost immediately, more vomit erupted from her mouth.

Although Beckett knew the Body Farm to be an invaluable resource for forensic pathologists and medical examiners, he considered the notion that his residents weren't quite ready for it yet.

Maybe you are *getting soft, Beckett,* he thought.

Beckett turned back to the corpse, only this time he didn't see a man with a purple face, but Wayne Cravat.

And the bees weren't coming out of his chest, but the gash in his throat that Beckett had made with a scalpel.

"I'm fine now," Maria said, standing up straight. "I'll be fine."

To prove this point, she sipped some water and then defiantly held the rest of her stomach's contents at bay.

Beckett had to give the girl credit. You could knock her down, but she got right back up again.

"No maggots," Grant offered without context. "No flies."

Beckett's eyes darted from Dr. Swansea to Maria, back to Grant.

"Please excuse Grant here, sometimes his autism gets the best of him."

Grant shook his head.

"There are no maggots on the body. Blowflies usually lay eggs and maggots hatch within twenty-four hours out in the open here like this. There should be maggots feasting on this corpse. I'm guessing that it's the bees that are keeping them away."

"Bravo," Dr. Swansea said. "There was a body found in a peach grove in Georgia a few years ago. The corpse was very close to a massive beehive—not in the body, mind you, but nearby—and there were some serious doubts about the actual time of death. The body was also hanging as you see here, which messes with the usual lividity that one might expect to see."

"Which is why you ran this experiment."

Beckett nodded; he had figured this out, of course. Grant was bright, he'd give him that, but Beckett was smarter.

Well, maybe not, he admitted. *But definitely more handsome.*

"All right, what's next?" Beckett asked, casting a wistful glance in Maria's direction. Her face had turned a shade of white reminiscent of a used condom left out in the sun. "I think I'm allergic to bees—let's get the hell out of here."

Chapter 11

"WHAT'S WITH THE CAGE?" Pedro asked as they stepped into the clearing.

It was wetter here, and Dr. Swansea explained that this was on purpose. They had specifically grown trees with thick, nearly impenetrable canopies. As a result, the area beneath, in which they stood, was unusually warm and muggy. The ground was also soft, and the cage that Pedro was referring to was half-buried in mud. At about two feet high, four feet wide, and eight feet long, the cage wiring was covered in blue plastic, likely to keep it from rusting.

"To keep the predators out," Grant answered. This was, of course, the right answer, and Dr. Swansea quickly confirmed it.

"That's right; occasionally we take measures to keep the raccoons and other wildlife away from the corpses. The wind's blowing now, but usually this entire farm smells rank, a not so subtle advertisement to animals that a buffet awaits. Most of the time, we let the native creatures run wild, do their thing, but sometimes we want to look for something specific."

"Like bees," Maria offered.

"Yeah, like bees."

Beckett stepped forward, then dropped on his haunches and peered into the muck. At first blush, the ground only appeared to be covered in a layer of soggy leaves. But the longer you stared, the more the shape of a body started to appear.

The corpse was discolored and blended almost seamlessly into the earth. It was also teeming with insects.

"And in this case, we wanted to see how insects behave when the body is partly submerged in mud."

Beckett was leaning close to the body when the corpse's fingers twitched, and he stumbled backward.

Dr. Swansea laughed.

"As you can see, the beetles are having a feast today."

"What do you mean, a partly submerged body? Do insects act differently below or above ground inside a corpse?" Pedro asked.

"Indeed, they do. Look, come on over here to the empty plot and I'll show you," Dr. Swansea instructed, moving away from the first body. "When you do a residency placement here, we'll go over everything. We examine every square inch of the bodies and the earth around them, scouring it for clues, remains, debris, insect life, soil pH, you name it. We document it all. Since the Body Farms' inception, we've studied more than five hundred bodies, and have performed more than two hundred individually designed experiments."

Dr. Swansea gestured toward a cage that was a twin to the first one, only there was no body buried beneath. Beckett was nearly sure of it.

"Beckett, give me a hand here and we'll lift it up," Dr. Swansea said.

Beckett nodded and stepped forward. Together, the two of them managed to lift one side, using the other as a hinge embedded in the earth. It was far heavier than Beckett had expected.

"Go ahead," Swansea instructed. "Feel how wet the earth is under there, how deep you can sink in."

At first, nobody moved. But Trevor eventually got up the nerve and cautiously poked a finger into the earth. He pushed it in about an inch, then sprang to his feet.

"Oh, come on, *feel* the earth. Feel the difference in temperature relative to the outside air."

"You sure there's no body under there?" Trevor asked, a slight tremor to his voice.

Dr. Swansea shook his head.

"You really are one of Beckett's students, aren't you? No, son, there's no body under there."

Trevor suddenly got on all fours and started to push his gloved hands into the muck. He made it to the second knuckle before he met resistance.

"Keep going, you can keep going," Dr. Swansea urged.

Everyone fell silent, rapt by the strangely hypnotic scene of Trevor's hands sinking into the mud. It was only then that Beckett realized that his phone was ringing in his pocket.

Under normal circumstances, he wouldn't even have the damn thing turned on. But after what had happened with Yasiv and the whole missing body fiasco, Beckett thought it prudent to stay abreast of any new developments.

Without thinking, he reached into his pocket and pulled it out.

"He's dead," a female voice said flatly.

Beckett's blood ran cold and he stepped away from the body cage and his residents.

This was it. This was the ransom call he'd been expecting. Whoever had taken the body was now calling with their demands.

Money.

Power.

Something.

"Dr. Campbell?"

He heard his voice in stereo and turned to see a red-faced Dr. Swansea calling to him.

"Yes?" he gasped.

"I can't—it's too heavy. Beckett, I—"

The cage suddenly came crashing down, pinning Taylor beneath it, pushing his face and chest into the warm mud.

Taylor screamed, but Beckett still didn't move.

"What do you want?" he hissed into the phone.

"Dr. Campbell, it's Delores. My father… he's dead. He's been murdered."

Chapter 12

"DELORES?" BECKETT REPEATED, PRESSING a finger into his opposing ear, and walked further away from the commotion behind him. "Who killed *who*? What are you talking about?"

In the back of his mind, a small voice reminded him what the temporary secretary had said about Delores taking a personal leave.

"My dad... he went in to get a degenerative disk in his neck repaired and according to the surgeon, everything went okay. But after being sent home, the pain just kept getting worse. Then he started shaking, so I took him into the 'merge. It was too late. He... he *died*."

Beckett shook his head, trying to clear his thoughts. This only served to give him another headache.

"I'm not sure I understand. Can you slow down and start from the beginning?"

Delores was breathing heavily on the other end of the line and it took her a moment to regain some semblance of calm.

"I'm sorry, I didn't know who else to call. About a week ago, my father had surgery to fix a compressed disk in his neck. He was weak after the surgery, which I was told would improve over time. But he never got better, and today he started trembling, so I took him into the ER. He had a seizure right there in the car, and another one in the hospital. Then his heart just stopped. He died. It's—it's not okay, it's not right, Dr. Campbell. My dad... he was perfectly healthy, and the surgeon said there was zero risk to the surgery. *Zero.*" Delores started to sob. "I don't know what to do."

Beckett's eyes narrowed.

"He said that? The surgeon said there was no risk?"

"Yes," Delores managed. "He said it was a completely safe procedure."

This got Beckett's attention; *all* surgeries carried risks, no matter how minor, just like all drugs had potential side-effects. To say otherwise was, at best, a bare-faced lie.

"Okay, I'm coming in. You at NYU?"

"Yeah, I'm here. I'm trying to get some answers, but no one's talking to me. It's like—it's like they don't even care that he's dead!"

"Calm down, Delores; try your best to just stay calm. I'm about an hour away and I'm coming there right now."

"What—what do you want me to do while I wait?"

Beckett thought about this for a moment.

"Just stay there, and whatever you do, don't let them take your father's body to the morgue."

Delores started to say something else, but Beckett cut her off.

"I'll be an hour—just stay put."

He hung up the phone and turned back to his residents.

What the fuck?

His jaw immediately went slack.

It looked as if a corpse had risen from the dead; the man emerging from the cage had mud coating his arms and chest, and there were leaves on his face and in his hair.

"Oh my—"

The undead suddenly leaped at Beckett, reaching for him with earthy, greasy fingers.

Beckett stepped backward, and the corpse tripped and fell.

"You asshole," the zombie screamed. "You *asshole!*"

Beckett blinked three times before realizing that the corpse was actually Taylor.

And then he burst out laughing. He laughed for a good thirty seconds, before stopping when he realized that no one else had joined in.

Not even Dr. Swansea.

"Shit, I'm sorry," he said, stifling another chuckle. "I had a call... it was important. Seriously."

Several of the other residents helped Taylor to his feet and were now holding him back.

"You did that on purpose!" the man shouted, mud spraying from his lips.

Beckett shook his head.

"No, it was an accident—I got a call. *You* saw me get a call. A friend... a friend's father just died."

He looked to Dr. Swansea for support, but there was only a hardness in the man's eyes.

"Back me up here... I mean, uhh, at least we know what happens to a body when it rises out of the muck. That's experiment... what? Two hundred and one? That has some value, right?"

This infuriated Taylor even further, and he once again tried to come for Beckett. He was so incensed that it took three residents to keep him from breaking free.

"I'm sorry, I really am," Beckett began candidly. "It was an accident—I didn't mean to drop the cage. And I'll get you a new T.J. Maxx outfit, promise. Right now, though, I gotta take off. I gotta get back to the city."

Dr. Swansea gave him a curious look.

"No, for real. I wasn't joking about that; a friend's father just died."

"What do you want us to do?" Grant asked. He wasn't one of the residents holding Taylor back, Beckett noted.

"We should get the fuck out of here and report him to the medical board, that's what we should do," Taylor spat.

Beckett glowered at the resident for a moment, but then he relaxed and took a deep breath.

"If that's what you want to do, go for it. But I've got tenure. Either way, I really must get going. You guys can either take the rest of the day off, or you can stay here and learn. If that's okay by you, Dr. Swansea."

The man scratched his beard.

"I can move some things around to make room. What I've shown you guys so far is only the beginning. I have dozens of fascinating cases that would be of interest to any forensic pathologist."

"See? It's all for the best." Beckett was going to leave it at that and head back to the building to change out of the hazmat suit, before reconsidering. "Taylor, I really am sorry. It was an honest accident."

"It's Trevor, you asshole."

Beckett cringed and bit his tongue.

Within five minutes, he was back in his street clothes. Three minutes after that, Beckett was back on the road, driving to meet a hysterical Delores who had just lost her father.

And goddammit, if that black car wasn't following him again.

PART II

Missing Body

Chapter 13

SERGEANT HENRY YASIV SAT at his desk and tapped his pencil incessantly. He'd been doing this for the better part of an hour, all the while staring at the phone on his desk.

Three times Detective Dunbar had come into the room and asked him if everything was all right, and all three times Sergeant Yasiv had grunted an affirmative.

But it wasn't true.

He *wasn't* all right. In fact, he was far from it.

"Fuck it," he muttered, finally grabbing the phone and bringing it to his ear. He dialed the number that was scratched on the pad now stippled with pencil marks. It rang once, twice, then a female voice answered.

"SVU, how may I direct your call?"

"Yeah, I'm looking for a Detective Crumley," Yasiv said, trying to keep his voice calm and even despite his roiling emotions.

"He's busy at the moment, may I take a message?"

"Can you let him know that Sergeant Yasiv called?"

He was met only by silence.

"Hello?"

"Sergeant Yasiv, I'm going to put you through. He's been expecting your call," the female voice replied.

"Expecting my call? Why—" but the line clicked and then started to ring again.

"Yasiv, it's good to hear from you. What can I help you with?" Detective Crumley asked.

All this happened so quickly that Sergeant Yasiv was flustered, and it took him a moment to collect his thoughts.

"Yeah, well, I was hoping... you know that search warrant that you helped me get before?"

"Yes."

Crumley was hesitant, which wasn't a good sign.

"You think you can help me get it expanded?"

The man cleared his throat before answering and Yasiv knew what he was going to say.

"That will be... problematic."

Sergeant Yasiv frowned.

"Problematic? Why?"

The detective sighed.

"The Wayne Cravat case has been shut down on our end, Sergeant."

Yasiv couldn't believe his ears. The DA had made it absolutely clear not two weeks ago that finding Wayne Cravat was a priority.

"What do you mean, shut down?"

"After the indictment against Brent Hopper, the DA decided that the case was closed."

"Closed? *Closed?* You can't be serious."

Yasiv was incredulous, but he wasn't surprised. Wayne Cravat had essentially been cleared twice: once by a jury, and then by him, Dunbar, and Crumley, collectively. The man had nothing to do with Bentley Thomas's murder. And because of that, the DA couldn't use him to garner any positive press. Instead, the man's case had essentially become a land mine, what with the botched arrest and subsequent trial, that everyone wanted to steer clear of.

Everyone but Yasiv, because he knew that the man was dead.

And that Dr. Beckett Campbell had killed him.

"Closed," Crumley confirmed. "Hopper struck a deal, rolled over on Winston Trent. He's going to serve a minimum of twenty years. As for Wayne... the DA managed to lift his parole and bury his past transgressions. Just isn't worth expending the resources chasing an innocent man who never should have been charged in the first place."

Yasiv began tapping his pencil again, this time holding it like a cigarette that he desperately wanted.

What a fucking mess. If it hadn't been for Wayne Cravat, I would never have found out about Beckett—about the real *Dr. Beckett Campbell.*

"Shit."

"Hank, fair warning, the DA told me explicitly to shut this down. He didn't send one of his minions, or an email, or even call me. He came to me in person, which has only happened a handful of times since I started in the SVU. My advice? Let it go."

Yasiv tapped the pencil so hard that the tip broke and tore through several sheets of yellow paper.

"Let it go? I'm not gonna let it go. Wayne didn't just disappear; he was murdered. So, no, I don't care what the DA says, there's no way am I letting this go."

There was a short pause.

"Detective Crumley, you still there?"

"I'm sorry, Sergeant Yasiv," Crumley said in a tone that was unusually professional. "I can't help you out. But again, as a friend, I suggest you focus your attention elsewhere."

"This is bullshit," Yasiv muttered. When there was no reply, he repeated the words, louder this time. "This is bullshit!"

"Let it go," Crumley said one final time before hanging up.

"*This is bullshit!*"

Yasiv slammed the phone down hard in its cradle.

While he was still stewing, Detective Dunbar poked his head into Yasiv's office for the fourth time that morning.

"Hank? You okay?"

Yasiv looked up at his friend with blazing eyes.

"No, I'm not fucking okay, Dunbar. I'm not okay, and I won't let this go!"

Chapter 14

IT DIDN'T TAKE BECKETT an hour to make it to the hospital, but just over half that time. This was mostly due to the fact that he was trying to shake the black car that followed him.

Beckett was more convinced than ever that this was an undercover officer sent by Yasiv to try to find out where he'd stashed Wayne Cravat's body.

If only I knew, Beckett thought as he parked and then hurried into the hospital.

It was coming up on midday now, and it was unseasonably warm outside. Sweat had already started to bead on his forehead and made his polo shirt stick to the small of his back.

"Hi, I'm looking for Delores Leacock," Beckett informed the Surgical Department secretary. He wiped the sweat away with a tattoo-covered forearm while he waited for her to reply.

"I'm sorry, but we don't have anybody by that name here," the woman, who was a carbon copy of the temp who had taken over for Delores in the Pathology Department, informed him.

Beckett rolled his eyes.

"No, she wasn't a patient, it was her father. He was here having surgery on his neck—disk fusion—and something went wrong."

"What's his name?"

"Mr. Leacock."

The response failed to impress the woman.

"I'm sorry sir, but we do not give out patient information."

"What the—? I'm not looking for patient information, I'm looking for Mr. Leacock." He shook his head. "I'm a doctor;

Dr. Beckett Campbell, Forensic Pathology... tenured professor at NYU."

The woman not so subtly glanced at the tattoos on his arms, then looked up at his spiky blond hair.

"I'm sorry, sir; do you have any ID on you?"

Beckett, scowling now, tapped his back pocket. His wallet wasn't there; he must have left it in the car.

"No, I don't. Let me guess, you're a temp? Yes? No? Well, if not, your position will become temporary if you don't tell me where—"

A flicker of movement in his periphery caught his attention, and Beckett turned to see an absurdly tall security guard approaching.

"Everything okay here?" the man asked in a baritone voice.

"Yeah, everything's fine, Lurch," Beckett replied, looking back at the secretary. "I need to know if Mr. Leacock's body is still here."

The woman crossed her arms over her chest defiantly.

Very mature, Beckett thought.

"Excuse me, sir, would you please take a seat?" Lurch asked, his voice completely devoid of intonation.

"No," Beckett shot back, "I'm not taking a seat. I need to know if—"

A commotion from down the hall caused Beckett to stop mid-sentence.

"Please, the body needs to stay here... it's my father, *please*," a distraught woman pleaded.

"Delores!" Beckett shouted. Delores was a big woman, and she was tightly gripping to the rail of a gurney that three orderlies were struggling to wheel down the hall. Even though the gurney was covered in a sheet, he recognized the unmistakable outline of a body beneath.

Beckett took a single step in her direction when a hand came down on his shoulder. He immediately whipped around and glared at the Addams' Family manservant.

The security guard swallowed visibly and then released his hold and took a step backward.

Beckett returned his attention to Delores.

"Hold on," he shouted, moving toward the trio of orderlies. "Just hold the fuck up. What's your hurry, anyway? It's not like the guy's going anywhere."

Chapter 15

"FIRST, I WANT TO apologize for the way you were treated, Dr. Campbell."

Beckett waved the man's apology away.

"Fine—it's fine, but maybe you should think about using another company for your temp secretaries."

"Yes, well, hospital and university policies dictate that staff are required to have their identification on them at all times," the man said.

Beckett made a face.

After the altercation in the hallway, he'd successfully convinced the orderlies to call their boss and keep the body where it was. The last thing that Beckett wanted was for the body to go to the morgue. Once it arrived there, it became the property of another department, which meant identifying Mr. Leacock's surgeon would mean navigating through a lot of red tape.

"What did you say your name was again?"

"My name is Pete Trout and I am the Assistant Manager of the Patient Crisis Awareness Division of the Human Resources Department."

Beckett shook his head.

"Is that a title or a dissertation? The Crisis Patient—never mind. Look, I want to speak to the surgeon who operated on Mr. Leacock."

Now it was Pete Trout's turn to shake his head.

"I'm sorry but I cannot divulge that information, as you well know, being a staff member here." Beckett started to say something, but the man cut him off, "But as you also know, Dr. Campbell, whenever there is a death in one of our operating rooms, an investigation is automatically initiated."

"Yeah, I know, but what I also know," Beckett began, casting a furtive glance over at Delores who was dabbing her mascara-smeared eyes, "is that these investigations usually amount to Jack fucking shit. In the highly unusual event that something is learned from your little dog and pony show, y'all tend to just keep it to yourself."

He had to give Pete Trout credit; the Assistant Manager of Colostomy Complaints managed to keep a straight face. The corners of his lips didn't even so much as twitch.

"With all due respect, Dr. Campbell, I don't tell you how to do your job, and I'd appreciate it if you didn't tell me how to do mine."

"That's what you call what you're doing? A job? I beg—"

Once again, Pete Trout cut him off.

"But, given the circumstances and your very close relationship with the deceased, I will make a note to keep you apprised of the situation. As you know, however, there are certain things that occur at the hospital that are kept in house, and for good reason."

The comment caught Beckett off guard. He couldn't be sure, but he thought that this might be an underhanded reference to the fact that his tribunal regarding Craig Sloan had been kept out of the press.

Everyone has their secrets, Pete, and I'll find yours.

Frowning now, Beckett rose to his feet and indicated for Delores to do the same.

"Okay, fine. I give up. But I'll take the body, though. After all, it belongs to the Pathology Department now."

Beckett offered his best smug expression as he turned toward the door, only to be drawn back again by Peter Trout's sleepy voice.

"Oh, I'm sorry, Dr. Campbell, I forgot to mention that Mr. Leacock's body has already been assigned to a pathologist."

Beckett was incredulous.

"What? Who?"

For a split-second, he thought he caught a hint of a smile cross the douchebag's lips, but then it was gone.

"Dr. Karen Nordmeyer. Do you know her?"

Chapter 16

"I'M GOING OUTSIDE FOR a smoke. When I get back, I want all detectives in the conference room," Sergeant Yasiv ordered.

Dunbar stared at him for a moment, blinking like a fish out of water.

"Are you going to tell me what's going on? Does this have anything to do with Brent Hopper or Wayne Cravat?"

"Just do it, Dunbar," Yasiv snapped, immediately regretting his tone. Dunbar wasn't at fault here. He was just trying to be a good person, a good friend, which Yasiv knew him to be.

They'd been through a lot together, and with Damien Drake's help, they'd collaborated to bring down the mayor and dozens of corrupt cops. Not bad for two inexperienced boys in blue.

"I'm sorry, just get everyone together, please."

Dunbar's face went hard, then he nodded and left the room.

Yasiv followed him out, but instead of heading towards the conference room, he left through the front doors and immediately lit a cigarette.

As he stood under the shadow of 62nd precinct, he thought back to his meteoric rise from police officer to sergeant.

Mayor Ken Smith had been in charge when Yasiv joined the force, pulling the strings as he saw fit. After Detective Damien Drake had gotten rid of the old sergeant—Sergeant Rhodes—Chase Adams had been promoted, but she'd quickly moved on to the FBI after only a few months. Then, when hints of corruption in the NYPD started making the news, Mayor Smith had no choice but to hire somebody who was clean as a whistle, someone with an impeccable track record.

Someone who was green and naïve.

Someone who the mayor could manipulate and control.

And that someone just happened to be named Henry Yasiv.

But Ken Smith's plan had backfired; instead of settling things down, with Drake and his PI firm's help, Yasiv had brought the Mayor's entire cabinet to its knees.

Even Dr. Beckett Campbell had lent a hand.

But that was then, and this was now.

Yasiv finished his cigarette, then immediately lit another.

It started with Craig Sloan; Beckett had claimed that he'd killed the man in self-defense, and while his account of events had raised many red flags, the doctor had gotten a pass.

But that was just the beginning. Ever since that day, those who got close to the man, especially people with troubled pasts of their own, ended up dead shortly thereafter.

For instance, there was the evidence that Dr. Karen Nordmeyer had given him regarding Beckett's DNA being found under Bob Bumacher's nails. Couple this with the photograph found at Winston Trent's house printed on special paper from the Pathology Department, and the pastor who ID'd Beckett, and a fairly firm case could be made.

None of these things were smoking guns, but collectively? Either Beckett had a horrible string of bad luck, or he was involved in these unfortunate 'accidents.'

And Yasiv couldn't get the mystery of what happened to Captain Loomis—the man had been shot dead just before Yasiv and his crew had come to arrest him—out of his mind.

Could that have been Beckett, too? Could he be on a rampage, taking out all the scum living in New York City?

Yasiv sighed.

Maybe I should just let this go like Crumley suggested.

He took a heavy haul on his smoke then flicked the butt to the ground. On the way back to his office, the conference room door opened, and Dunbar peered out.

"Sergeant?" he said, his eyes soft.

"Yeah, what is it, Dunbar?"

Yasiv was tired. He didn't sleep well anymore, not after the horrible things he'd seen. An occupational hazard, to be sure, but not one that he'd come to grips with yet.

It was the bad dreams, mostly. He wasn't sure when they'd started — it was either after discovering the man who'd been electrocuted with a car battery, or the Download Killer's first victim in the barn — but they seemed to fill his head every night.

Yasiv recalled the way that Drake had looked at him outside the barn, and even though the man hadn't said so, it was clear that he didn't think Yasiv had the chops to cut it as a detective.

Maybe Drake was right, Yasiv thought. *But I'm not a detective anymore.*

I'm a sergeant.

"I've rounded up the detectives as you asked — they're all waiting for you in here," Dunbar informed him.

With a heavy sigh, Sergeant Yasiv nodded and stepped into the room.

All eyes were on him as he made his way to the front and then started to pace.

He did this for a good thirty seconds, still mulling over what to do next.

Let it go. Beckett was good to you, he helped you, he was a friend. He's not like these other criminals. This is New York City, for Christ's sake, there's a murder almost every day that you can focus your attention on.

Just let it go.

Yasiv reached for the closest computer and quickly loaded the browser. He was aware that everyone was still staring at him, more than a few eyebrows raised, but he didn't care.

Because the truth was, it didn't matter that, until recently, Beckett had been his friend or that the man was a respected doctor. It didn't even matter that Beckett had helped oust Mayor Ken Smith and bury his corrupt corporation.

It didn't matter, because the NYPD was done with corruption, with backhanded favors, with letting people off a sinking ship.

That's how a mayor like Ken Smith came into power and almost crippled the entire city in the first place.

Gritting his teeth, Yasiv spun the computer around, revealing a photograph of Beckett taken from his University ID.

"This is Dr. Beckett Campbell, Senior Medical Examiner for New York State," he said, his eyes blazing into Dunbar's as he spoke. "And he's the prime suspect in at least three murders. I want you to put a hold on all your other cases; I want Dr. Campbell to be your primary focus moving forward."

Chapter 17

"DELORES, MAYBE YOU SHOULD just go home," Beckett said, laying a hand on her shoulder. "Take as much time off as you want or need. I'm assuming that your dad had a will?"

Delores wiped at her eyes and sniffed.

"Yeah, my stepmother took care of all that. I just don't... I don't understand what happened. It was supposed to be routine surgery. I never thought he would *die*."

Beckett nodded sympathetically.

Despite the surgeon's claim that Mr. Leacock's surgery was risk-free, sometimes bad things just happened. Sometimes there were complications with the anesthesia, or an undiagnosed heart condition that reared its ugly head. But considering that Beckett hadn't even seen the body yet—it was still covered by a sheet that was judicially protected by the three orderlies—he couldn't say for certain if anything malicious had taken place.

But no matter what happened, Delores being here wasn't going to help. Emotions at a time like this only served to muddy the waters.

"I promise I'll do whatever I can to find out what happened to your dad."

Delores finally relented.

"I know you will, Beckett. I know you will."

Beckett inspected her for a moment, making sure at the same time to keep pace with the gurney, which was evidently operated by three orderlies named Earnhardt, Hamilton, and Schumacher. Even Lurch the security guard was having a hard time staying with them, despite his three-acre strides.

"If there's anything you need, please just call. I mean it."

Delores nodded again, and Beckett motioned toward the bay of civilian elevators to their right. Shoulders slumped, the woman walked over to them and pressed the down button. Just as the silver box pinged announcing its arrival, a thought occurred to Beckett.

"One more thing, Delores, do you know the name of the doctor that performed your dad's surgery?"

Delores slid a hand between the elevator doors, keeping it open.

"Yeah, it was Dr. Gourde."

Beckett's brow knitted.

"Gourde?"

"Gourde."

"Like those retarded little pumpkins?"

Delores made a face and Beckett shook his head.

"Don't worry about it. Go get some rest and be with your family. I'll find him."

Lewis Hamilton took a corner with the gurney and, not wanting to let it out of his sight, Beckett redoubled his pace, ignoring the sweat that continued to soak his shirt. For all he knew, Dr. Karen Nordmeyer would steal this body like she'd stolen Wayne's corpse, and he would never see it again.

Eventually, they came to a more discrete single elevator that required a key card to operate. One of the orderlies swiped his and the elevator started its ascent from the basement. While they waited for it to arrive, Beckett deliberately positioned himself between the orderlies and the security guard. When it pinged, Beckett waited for the orderlies to push the gurney inside, then followed them in. Just before Lurch could enter, however, he pointed over the man's shoulder, his eyes going wide.

"Oh my god, can you do that in here?"

The security guard frowned and turned.

"Do what?"

"Vape in a hospital—what's this world coming to when these damn hipsters can do whatever they want just because they're wearing suspenders."

"What? Where?" the security guard demanded.

Beckett gently eased him into the hallway and then pointed.

"There!"

The man took two steps forward and the elevators doors started to close. Beckett smiled; he'd timed his ruse perfectly.

Hearing the mechanical whir of the doors, the security guard whipped around and reached out, but he was too late. A split second before they closed, Beckett made two 'V' symbols with his fingers on opposing hands and then inserted one into the other.

"Vape Nation," he mouthed. And then the door closed.

Finally alone with the orderlies, Beckett looked down at the body on the gurney.

"I'm just gonna take a wee little peek here under the sheets, I hope you don't mind."

He paused, giving them an opportunity to protest. But it appeared that now, with the security guard gone, and finding themselves trapped in a steel box with a unique looking doctor with blond hair and tattoos covering his arms, they'd suddenly lost their nerve.

Nobody said anything.

Beckett reached down and pinched the corner of the sheet, then slowly pulled it back. He didn't need to lift it very far.

Mr. Leacock's skin had already started to turn gray and his eyelids had retracted. There was a goiter on the side of his neck that was so large that it distorted his neck and jaw.

"Jesus."

Beckett reached out and pressed against the mass, and his fingers sank in a little. When he pulled his hand away, the indentions remained for a moment before slowly filling with fluid.

"I don't think you should do that."

Beckett's eyes flicked up and he stared at the orderly who looked all of fourteen years old.

He thought about intimidating the man-child but decided against it. He had enough enemies as it was.

"You're probably right; I don't mind waiting for my dear friend Dr. Nordmeyer to do her dirty work."

With that, Beckett replaced the sheet over the man's head and then started to whistle as the elevator descended into the basement.

Down to the place where ghosts were born.

Chapter 18

EXHAUSTED NOW, YASIV HEADED outside for another cigarette. He felt dirty, but, paradoxically, part of him also felt cleansed.

The task of eliminating corruption within the ranks of the NYPD had extended to making sure that nobody got a pass when it came to crime, even if they were well connected. Which meant that he wasn't going to 'let it go' when it came to Dr. Beckett Campbell.

But still, sometimes even doing the right thing came with feelings of regret and remorse.

Yasiv had just put a smoke to his lips when the door flung open and Dunbar burst out.

"You can't be serious about this," he exclaimed, his eyes blazing.

Yasiv cupped the end of his cigarette and lit it.

"Does it look like I'm joking?"

"But... Beckett? He's one of us, he's one of our friends. He's been Drake's friend forever, and—"

"And where is Drake now, Dunbar? Have you heard from him? He's supposed to be our almighty Savior, the person who'd brought down the mayor and ANGUIS Holdings, but not only is he not in New York, he's not even in the country."

Dunbar's eyes bulged.

"He can't—you know why he isn't here. If Drake steps foot on American soil, he'll be thrown in jail. That dickhead Kramer won't let up—"

Yasiv felt anger building inside him now, and he tried his best to keep it at bay. Dunbar's refrain was all too common: a plethora of reasons *not* to pursue someone, all the while ignoring the most important fact.

"I showed you guys the evidence in there, the links between Beckett and Winston Trent, Wayne Cravat, Bob Bumacher, and Captain Loomis. And you wanna know what happened? Not a single one of you said, hey, sergeant, this doesn't fit, your logic is flawed, the evidence isn't telling enough. We've gone after people with less, you *know* that, Dunbar. You're just letting your friendship cloud your judgment."

Now it was Dunbar who became enraged, throwing his hands up, his face turning red.

"Friendship? Let me tell you a little about friendship, Hank. We came up, together. Me and you both followed in Drake's footsteps, and along the way, when we needed Beckett, he was there for us. All those guys—Screech, Beckett, Drake, Chase, Hanna, and even Leroy—we're in this together. We brought down the mayor. We brought down a multi-million-dollar organization that was importing heroin into the city… we can't just pretend that didn't happen–or I can't, at least. You helped Drake, you helped Screech. But now… now you're on a witch hunt for Beckett? Why?"

Yasiv exhaled a thick cloud of smoke.

"Yeah, we did all that, sure, I won't deny it. But now that we've taken out the garbage, what are we supposed to do? Just let it pile up again? Clog the streets and sewers? What happens during the next mayoral election? Have you thought about that? We keep going this way, and the next person in charge will be even worse, even more corrupt than Ken Smith. And I won't stand for it; no way, not after all the work we put in. Beckett or no Beckett, Doctor, Lawyer, fucking priest, I don't care. I'm just following the evidence."

Dunbar's anger seemed to have transitioned into something else now. He lowered his eyes and then reached into his pocket. Before Yasiv could get a handle on what was happening, the detective was holding his badge in one hand, his service pistol in the other.

"What's this?" Yasiv demanded.

"It's my resignation."

"Oh, grow up, Dunbar. You're not resigning. You want that job in the SVU? Beckett's case is linked to Wayne and Winston. Bringing him down will go a long way to getting your foot in the door over there. And that's what you really want, isn't it?"

"Take it," Dunbar said, his eyes welling with tears.

"No—I won't."

Dunbar surprised Yasiv by thrusting both objects at his chest. Yasiv managed to grab the gun, but the man's badge slipped to the ground.

"Think about what you're doing, Dunbar. Think long and hard."

"I have—I've resigned. And now, I want you to arrest me."

"*What*?" Yasiv balked. "What the hell are you talking about?"

"Arrest me."

"Arrest you? For what? Have you lost your fucking mind, Dunbar?"

"No, I haven't. But if you're going after Beckett, you might as well start with me; I broke about a half a dozen laws trying to bring down the mayor and ANGUIS Holdings—in the very least, I'm guilty of computer fraud, hacking, that sort of shit. So, arrest me."

A headache started to build behind Yasiv's eyes now.

"Give me a break here, Dunbar."

"No, I'm not giving you a break. Like you said, nobody's getting breaks anymore. I want you to fucking arrest me, Hank. I plead guilty to cyberfraud."

Yasiv shook his head back and forth, not believing what he was hearing.

Dunbar was one of the very few men he could still trust in the NYPD. Even after they'd cleaned out the department, he knew that the remaining officers looked at him a certain way. He wasn't exactly what one would consider a snitch, but he was something close to it.

"Come on, Dunbar. What Beckett's done… that's not looking up information on a computer without a warrant. That's murder… that's—"

Dunbar suddenly strode forward and jabbed a finger directly in his chest. Yasiv was so surprised by this, that if it weren't for the wall behind him, he might've stumbled.

"Now who's playing favorites, Hank? Think about the things that you've done in your career that weren't exactly kosher. You aren't a saint. None of us are. We all had to get our hands a little dirty to get rid of Ken Smith. Remember that."

"Dunbar, please," Yasiv pleaded. But Dunbar had already turned and was striding away, having made no effort to get his badge or gun back. "Dunbar… *Dunbar!*"

Chapter 19

"Dr. Nordmeyer? We have your body," one of the orderlies stated as he stepped out of the elevator. "Dr. Nordmeyer?"

The woman emerged from the shadows like some sort of rat. Her dark hair was pulled up in a bun, revealing a set of large, pointy ears. Beckett half expected her to bring her wrists to her mouth and make squeaking sounds.

But when Dr. Nordmeyer saw Beckett, her expression went from rodent-like to reptilian.

"What are you doing here?" she demanded.

"We're just bringing the body, as requested," the orderly replied.

Karen's eyes didn't drift from Beckett's.

"It's so nice to see you again, Dr. Nordmeyer," he said with a smile. "Looking as friendly as usual, I might add."

The woman scowled.

"Dr. Nordmeyer? We just need you to sign here." The orderly extended a clipboard. Somehow, the woman managed to not only grab the clipboard but also scribble her initials on it without so much as a glance.

Maybe she's part iguana, Beckett thought, *or whatever the hell that lizard-thing is that can move its eyes independently of each other.*

"Dr. Campbell, what are you doing here?"

"Thank you, have a nice day," the orderly said, backing into the elevator with the others. It was clear that they just wanted to get the hell out of there as quickly as possible.

Without waiting for Beckett to answer, Dr. Karen Nordmeyer grabbed the gurney and started wheeling down the tile hallway towards one of the examination rooms.

"The deceased is the father of a friend of mine — my secretary, actually," Beckett said as he walked alongside the woman. "He was in apparently good health before a simple disk fusion surgery. I want to know how he died."

"Then you're going to have to wait for my final report," Dr. Nordmeyer snapped. She used her ID card to unlock the door at the end of the hallway. "And then you can go ahead and shit all over it."

Beckett chuckled and moved ahead of her to hold the door open.

"Oh, gee, let me get that for you, sweetheart."

Karen's scowl deepened, but she accepted the gesture and pushed the gurney through. And then they were no longer alone.

Mr. Leacock's gurney joined three others in the morgue: on the first lay a middle-aged woman, split from shoulder to sternum, while the two other cadavers were covered in sheets.

"Do you think I have a problem with you?" Beckett asked. "No, don't answer that. I *do* have a problem with you, but that's not the point here. That Armatridge case? You can't hold that against me. You made a mistake and I fixed it. I mean, I made a mistake, too, but I owned up to it."

"Is there anything else?"

"No, I'm all right. Actually, do you have any popcorn?" Beckett hopped up on an empty gurney. "Because I was thinking of waiting around while you perform Mr. Leacock's autopsy."

Karen's upper lip curled, and she picked up a bloody scalpel from her workstation.

For a brief second, just a fraction of a moment of an inkling of a scintilla of a millisecond, Beckett thought Dr. Nordmeyer was going to lunge at him with the blade. But instead, she used it to gesture at the woman with her innards on display.

"Friend or not, I have to perform the autopsies in the order that I received the bodies. This one here could take me—" she shrugged, "—at least five or six hours. You know, I want to take my time to make sure I don't make any more 'mistakes'. You never know when someone is going to be looking over your shoulder, second-guessing everything you do."

"Not a problem, I can wait. Actually, I cleared my schedule all week, so I'm good."

Ah, the beauty of having tenure, and everyone else being afraid of me because I'm a killer.

The truth was, however, Beckett didn't really have all the time in the world. There was another pressing issue that he had to attend to; mainly, figuring out where Wayne Cravat's corpse had wandered off to.

"I might not even get to it until tomorrow," Dr. Nordmeyer informed him.

"Fine by me," Beckett replied quickly. He tapped the metal gurney with his nub of a finger. "These are surprisingly comfortable."

Karen looked as if she wanted to say more when Beckett's phone buzzed in his pocket. It rattled against the gurney, making a strange sound reminiscent of chattering teeth.

He pulled it out and quickly answered.

"Where are you, Beckett?" a female voice demanded.

"Suzan, how nice—"

"Where are you?"

Beckett winked at Karen, who was trying her best not to appear interested in his call.

"I'm among friends, what's up?"

"Did you push Trevor into a cage at the Body Farm?"

Beckett swallowed hard and lowered his voice.

"Pushed him? Not technically, no."

Suzan sighed.

"Beckett, this is serious. You need to come to your office right away. Trevor's threatening to press charges. Haven't you seen enough of the police lately?"

Beckett suddenly slid off the gurney and he turned his back to Dr. Nordmeyer now.

"In all honesty, Suze, it was just an accident. I was... I was distracted and let go of the cage. I didn't mean it."

"Well, mean it or not, you better get your ass here now, unless you want that jerk-off Yasiv to come back. And this time he won't have a search warrant with him, but handcuffs."

"I'm pretty sure he also had handcuffs with him last time, too. But I don't think—Suze? Suze?"

Becket pulled the phone away from his ear and cursed when he saw that she'd already hung up. He tried to act natural, but Karen knew that something was up, and she was beaming.

"Family trouble?"

"Yeah, something like that." Beckett looked down at Mr. Leacock's outline, which was still covered by the damn sheet, then at the scalpel in Dr. Nordmeyer's hand. "You know what? Something did come up, and I need to skedaddle. Gotta rearrange my sock drawer. Look, I know you didn't like the fact that I went over that Armand Armatridge report. But bear in mind, that we both made mistakes. I corrected them, came up with the actual cause of death. You might not like the way I did it but trust me when I say that you don't want to make any mistakes with Mr. Leacock there."

Beckett paused.

"Trust me."

Before Karen could say anything, Beckett retreated to the elevator. Just as he was stepping inside, however, a thought occurred to him.

"Hey, doc, any undocumented bodies come in lately?"

Karen's eyes narrowed.

"Undocumented? Why? You lose one?"

The elevator doors closed before Beckett could figure out if Dr. Nordmeyer was just making a joke, or if there was a deeper meaning to her words.

If she was teasing him because she knew exactly where Wayne Cravat's corpse was.

Chapter 20

BECKETT KEPT HIS HEAD Beckett kept his head low as he passed the temporary secretary and hurried to his office, the door of which hung open.

On the way from the morgue, he pictured Suzan's face as she sat behind his desk, scowling and pinched. She was undoubtedly a pretty woman, but when she got angry…

Suzan looked exactly the way Becket imagined. What he hadn't expected, however, was that Taylor would also be in the office. There were still flecks of mud on his neck and jaw, but they had obviously been left there for emotional impact; the rest of him, including his outfit, was clean. Nor did Beckett expect to see Grant, who was standing with his hands behind his back against the opposing wall.

"Is this an intervention?" Beckett asked, hooking a thumb over his shoulder towards the door that he'd just barged through. "Because if it is, I just need to do one more line, then I'll pack my bags and go. One more line, that's all I need—I'll call Jeff VanVonderen myself. I have him on speed dial."

Suzan's face, which had been strained before, underwent several additional convolutions.

She was *pretty, officer, I swear it.*

"Sit down and close the door," she ordered.

Beckett immediately dropped his ass into the nearest empty chair.

"Okay, Trevor," Suzan began, "He's here now. Talk to him."

Beckett looked at the man, but Taylor quickly averted his eyes and shook his head.

"I'm not going to talk to him if he's just gonna make fun of me."

Beckett rolled his eyes, but Suzan shot him a look, and he regained his composure.

"He's not gonna make fun of you," Suzan said. "Are you, Dr. Campbell?"

Beckett crossed himself.

"I swear on my mother's soul; I will not make fun of you."

Another glare from Suzan and Beckett decided to take this a little more seriously. She was right, he couldn't afford to do anything that might get back to Sergeant Yasiv.

Until I find that goddamn body, that is.

"Taylor, it was an accident. I didn't mean to drop the cage on you."

Taylor finally mustered enough courage to look at him and Beckett knew that he would have to work hard to convince the man of anything. He was fuming.

"Look, Taylor, you see that secretary out there? She's not my regular secretary, is she?"

Taylor shrugged, and Beckett turned to Suzan and then to Grant.

"You guys both know Delores, right? Uhh, the big-boned woman who has been working the pathology desk for a quarter-century? The one with the photo of her with Chris Hemsworth facing out?"

Both of them nodded.

"Well, she's not out there today, because her father died. Not only that, but he died right here, in this hospital, after undergoing surgery only a week ago. She called me all distraught and asked for help. That's why I dropped the cage. Like I said, it was an accident."

Grant nodded, and while Beckett was grateful for the support, it didn't appear as if Taylor was buying the story.

"And what about the Bird Box Challenge, huh? Blindfolding us and having us feel random organs? Or how about getting us drunk the night before, then on our first day of residency, we're told to perform autopsies on a bunch of corpses. What about that? Was that just an accident, too?"

Beckett held his hands out, palms up.

"And what did I say at that first class, huh? Can't remember? Fine, then let me remind you: I said that I'm not like other professors. I told you that I wanted you to actually learn something, and not just read obsolete crap from a textbook. I also told you that if you didn't think you could hack it, you could walk away. I made that perfectly clear."

Taylor started to fidget, a clear indication that he was nearing his wit's end.

"Yeah, sure, but I didn't think you were gonna push me into a goddamn metal coffin. How was I supposed to know that? That's not unorthodox... it's abuse — assault."

"Whoa, first of all, I never pushed you. Secondly, I'd be careful about throwing out words that you don't understand. You're a doctor, remember, not a lawyer."

"This is—"

"No, look, I really am sorry about what happened. If you want, you can transfer to any other pathology program in the state. I'll give you my highest recommendation, for what it's worth. And that's a promise. But I'm not going to sit here and listen to any more of this *fucking* whining."

Taylor got to his feet, but Beckett wasn't quite done yet.

"I also guarantee that if you stay, you will learn more in these next five years than you will in a lifetime out in Albany or whatever rural community you set up shop. This is New York City... you want to learn about death? You want to learn about forensic pathology? There's nowhere else in the US like it. As for my methods? Sure, they're unorthodox, unconventional, crude even. But they're effective. I would put you and your colleagues up against any other pathology department in the state, and I guarantee you'd come out on top. Hell, you probably know more than half the pathology administrators or the professors out there. So, you've got a decision to make. Do you want to stay, or do you want to go to Albany and investigate the recent cow-tipping epidemic?"

With every additional word, Taylor's eyes drifted lower and lower. By the end of the diatribe, the man was staring at his toes.

"I want to stay," he said in a meek voice.

"Good," Beckett said with a genuine smile. He slapped the man on the back a little harder than he'd intended. "Now, tell us about the mud. Was it warm?"

Taylor's eyes shot up and Suzan shouted his name.

"Just kidding, Jesus Christ, lighten up, Taylor."

Taylor continued to look at him even as he made his way out of the office.

"Just one thing, Dr. Campbell."

Beckett sighed.

"What is it now?"

"My name isn't Taylor. It's Trevor."

Beckett nodded and started to close the door.

"Noted. Now get to class, Taylor. I don't want to see you back here whining because you missed your goddamn period."

Chapter 21

Now that there were just three of them in his office, Beckett got down to the real business at hand. He turned to Grant first.

"Grant, I was hoping you might be able to do me a favor. Just a small one."

"Of course, Dr. Campbell. What is it that you need?"

For you to stop acting like a robot.

Beckett shook his head.

"There's a doctor I need you to look into for me. Nothing too serious; I just want to know about his personal life, whether he's having an affair, how many surgeries he's performed, his connection with neo-Nazis, where he went to school, and, oh, how many people he's killed."

Grant made a face but eventually nodded, just as Beckett knew we would.

Scratch that; you can be a robot for another day or two.

"What's the doctor's name?"

"Dr. Gourde."

"Gourde? You mean like fruits of the *Cucurbitaceae* family, the ones covered in perithecioid apothecium?"

"Hmm, yeah, that's him. Weird, I said the exact same thing when I heard his name just a few hours ago. Anyways, look into him and see what you can come up with. Think you can do that?"

Grant nodded.

"Thanks."

Grant left, and Beckett reluctantly turned to face Suzan.

"And then there were two..."

"You really think that's a good idea? Grant's not your lackey, you know. He's your resident."

"What? I'm giving the man a chance to earn some extra credit."

Suzan sighed and rubbed her eyes.

"What's going on with you, Beckett?"

"What do you mean?"

"First, there's this shit at your house with the Sergeant, and now this thing with Trevor and Delores. Who the hell is this Dr. Gourde? You're running around like a chicken with its head cut off. This isn't like you."

Beckett couldn't agree more.

Normally he was calm, cool, and calculated. The few times he'd actually lost his shit, like with Bob Bumacher, he'd almost ended up dead.

She's right, Beckett realized. *I need to calm down, let all this blow over.*

"I'm just trying to help Delores out. She's pretty broken up about her dad dying, as you can imagine."

Suzan's eyes suddenly started to water, and Beckett went to her.

"Shit, I'm sorry, I didn't mean it that way. I really appreciate you helping me out with Taylor—"

"Trevor."

"—yeah, with *him*. I'll make it up to you. Tonight, I'll cook for us. Sous vide prime New York strip loin with yours truly. No interruptions, I promise."

Suzan frowned.

"Like you promised to take me on a real vacation? That kind of promise?"

Beckett tilted his head to one side.

"You got me there. No, seriously, this time. A real dinner. Just me and you."

Suzan suddenly got to her feet and Beckett took a step backward.

"Where are you going?"

"Class, Beckett. Unlike some of us, I gotta work."

"You mean you *want* to work. You don't *need* to work. You've got me and I got all them monies, more than enough to share. Flashy cars, gold grill. I gotcha, babe."

"Yeah, sure. Just make sure that dinner is ready for seven and that the Cîroc is on ice, DJ Khaled."

They both laughed, and Suzan left the office on a high note for once.

And then there was just one... the loneliest number in the alphabet. Or maybe that's zero—who knows; numbers aren't even in the alphabet, anyway, genius.

Tired now, Beckett slid behind his desk and slumped in his chair. It was still warm from Suzan, but she was lighter than he, and her ass had messed with his butt grooves. He shifted around in a failed attempt to get comfortable.

The chair wasn't great to begin with. The padding was too thin, the back too erect. It also smelled faintly of polyvinyl chloride.

Who do I have to sleep with around here to get a real chair?

It was still too early to kick off for the day, and with nothing better to do, he switched on his computer.

After dismissing a notification that he had seven-thousand two-hundred and twelve unread emails, Beckett remembered something that Grant had told him on the drive to the Body Farm.

Something about a Podcast digging into Alister Cameron's murder spree, and the events that led up to his disappearance.

Sure enough, there were several threads about the good reverend on Reddit, some of which did mention an upcoming podcast. Thankfully, his name didn't show up anywhere. Nor was there even a passing mention of a dangerously handsome doctor with tattoos.

"Finally, some good news on a shitty day."

Just to be sure, he navigated to YouTube and punched 'talking in tongues' into the search bar.

"Woah."

Beckett had opened Pandora's box, and he tried to close it by adding the date and location he'd visited Reverend Alister Cameron.

This narrowed the number of hits, but not by as many as he'd expected.

"Jesus, I guess people talk in tongues all the time. And here I am, thinking that tongues was only reserved for special occasions," he mumbled.

When he added the name Alister Cameron only a handful of videos showed up. On a whim, Beckett clicked the most popular one, a video that had already garnered over five thousand views, and a few seconds later, his jaw fell to the floor.

"Shit," he swore. "Shit, shit, shit. Shihhfff al-l-l-ll loool-l-ll-l praisssssss-s-se a-ll-l-l-l-l-lllaaaaaaaaah ll-ll-l-llllllooooll-l-lloolll-l-l."

Chapter 22

EVEN AFTER DUNBAR WAS good and gone, Sergeant Yasiv just stared at the man's gun and badge in his hands.

Maybe he's right... maybe this isn't the way to go about things. Maybe I should just forget about Beckett and focus on the other two dozen unsolved homicides on the board.

But he couldn't do that. He'd already told all of the detectives assigned to 62nd precinct to focus on the doctor. After the corruption sweep, the men were wary of Yasiv. If he backed down now, he'd never be able to gain their trust.

Scowling, Yasiv started back inside the precinct. He passed several officers on the way to his office, one of whom asked about Dunbar.

"Taking a personal day," Yasiv replied without looking up.

A day... yeah, that's it. Dunbar just nees to vent. He'll be back. He's probably sore that you took Detective Hamm with you instead of him to serve the search warrant on Beckett's place.

It was wishful thinking, of course; and Yasiv couldn't afford to lose *any* men, least of all Dunbar.

Back in his office, he decided to test himself, to see if what Dunbar had said about him just having a vendetta against Beckett was true, or if the evidence really did point at the doctor.

Yasiv pulled up everything he had on Beckett and generated an itemized list.

One. Bob Bumacher was viciously murdered in his home. Beckett's DNA was found under the man's nails.

Two. A photograph of Bentley Thomas was found at the scene of Winston Trent's supposed suicide. The photo was printed on paper obtained from the Department of Pathology at NYU Med.

Three. Beckett urges Dr. Karen Nordmeyer to sign off Winston's case and mark it as a suicide.

Four. Wayne Cravat is still missing, and Beckett was seen at the church where the man was seeking counseling. Beckett also spoke to Wayne's parole agent about the man prior to his disappearance.

Five. Captain Loomis' unsolved murder. ???

There was something else, too, something that Yasiv didn't feel comfortable writing down, but couldn't quite be dismissed, either: the look on Beckett's face when he served the man with the search warrant.

The doctor was hiding something.

Unfortunately, the warrant had been limited to items related to Wayne Cravat, and they'd found none—least of all his body.

"Did you really think that Beckett was stupid enough to keep the body of the person he's killed in his basement, Hank? Really?"

He shook his head.

Yasiv took a cigarette out of the pack and dangled it between two fingers.

Beckett... you were scared when I served you the warrant. But you were also surprised. So surprised that you dropped your bags.

Yasiv stopped playing with the cigarette.

They weren't normal bags, were they? They were travel bags. It was as if you were returning from a trip. But why would you go on a trip if you'd just killed Wayne Cravat? And where did you go?

Yasiv scratched his cheek, wondering if there was anything to this line of thinking.

Did you get rid of Wayne's body somewhere while on vacation?

This didn't make much sense, but if Beckett was behind Wayne's disappearance, then it didn't make sense for him to go on vacation, either.

The key, if there was one, was to find out where Beckett had gone, Yasiv thought.

And there was only one way to do that.

He shoved Dunbar's badge and gun into the top drawer of his desk and then turned off his computer monitor.

He was required to report Dunbar's resignation immediately, as per NYPD protocol, but if neither of them was here, nobody would be the wiser.

On the way to his car, Yasiv bumped into another officer, who waved at him and asked where he was going.

"School. I'm going back to school."

"What? What for?"

Yasiv got into his car, but before closing the door, he said, "To learn, to find things out. Why else does one go to school?"

Chapter 23

BECKETT'S NECK WAS SORE from a permanent cringe.

The video he'd found not only put him at the church with Reverend Alister Cameron, but it also showed him talking in tongues. At first blush, he was proud of his performance, but the repercussions of the video being public were too great to ignore.

Beckett immediately clicked the Report tab, but when a text box opened up asking him to write why the video was being flagged, he hesitated.

"Um…"

He debated writing something along the lines of the user hadn't obtained his permission prior to uploading the video but didn't think that this would result in a permanent ban. What with the ever-eavesdropping Alexa and Google Assistant in millions of homes across the US, privacy no longer seemed to be a hot-button issue for Americans. Not like it used to be, anyway.

Instead, he wrote, *religious insensitivity*. But Beckett quickly erased that, too. It wasn't specific, nor damning enough. He wanted this video gone as soon as possible, so he had to touch on the issue that made Americans so uncomfortable that their very souls quivered. Beckett needed to find something that would force YouTube to take the video down in a matter of hours and not months.

I've got it, Beckett thought, clapping his hands together. *Racism! This video is racist!*

His enthusiasm waned when he realized that so many people had called each other racist over the past few years that it no longer held the same meaning that it used to.

No, I've got to find something better, something more damning.

Beckett stared at the screen for a good five minutes while he mentally went over all the offensive things he'd ever been accused of, from sexism to ageism, ableism, fatism, smoking-ism, vape-ism, hoarder-ism, women who live with too many cats-ism, heightism... yes, even heightism. He was particularly proud of that last one: during the opening of a lecture on dwarfism, Beckett mentioned that he'd dated a midget once, but that it hadn't worked out.

They just didn't see eye to eye.

Evidently, jokes weren't jokes anymore. They were barbed insults, intent to pillage and destroy, to crush human souls in a way that only Satan would approve.

And then, in a stroke of genius of the likes of which he'd never had before, and might never have again, three golden words that seemed to encompass—no, not encompass, but might actually be the root cause of every single problem in America flashed in Beckett's mind: *inappropriate gender pronouns.*

Smiling now, Beckett wrote those loaded words and pressed enter, confident that within a few hours, the video would be gone and with it, a record of him ever being in South Carolina.

At least on YouTube, that is.

It was coming on three in the afternoon now, and Beckett's brain was tired—he was done for the day. After peeling his body out of his uncomfortable chair, Beckett left his office, jokingly asking the temp to hold his calls for the day as he passed.

She predictably replied that she wasn't *his* secretary, to which Beckett shot back, *and you never will be!*

And then he went home to search for a missing body.

Chapter 24

SERGEANT HENRY YASIV'S PLAN, if you could call it that, was to ask the head of the Pathology Department at NYU Medical, one Dr. Hollenbeck, about Beckett's recent absences. He intended to do so under the guise of shoring up some details concerning a recent murder case.

A stretch, but not technically a lie.

Eventually, after following a series of arrows more complicated and circuitous than an IKEA showroom, Yasiv stumbled upon the Pathology Department.

Worried that Beckett might be around and not wanting another confrontation, he cautiously approached the departmental secretary. Unfortunately, she snapped her gum with unprecedented voracity as if to signify his arrival. It was almost as if the woman was timing each successive pop with his footsteps like the soundtrack to a bad Steve Martin movie.

"Hi," Yasiv said quietly.

The woman didn't raise her eyes from her computer; she just cracked her gum and nodded.

"Is this where… is this where Dr. Beckett Campbell works?"

"Uh-huh."

"Oh, okay, and what about Dr. Hollenbeck?"

The woman finally looked up.

"Are you the police or something?"

Yasiv started to pull his badge from his pocket.

"Well, actually…"

His ears suddenly perked; he could hear voices coming from down the hall. Familiar voices.

Beckett's voice—and Suzan's.

He tapped the desk.

"That's alright. You can get back to Candy Crush now."

The secretary shrugged and Yasiv retreated out of sight, but still within earshot.

Beckett was asking somebody to look up a doctor, a Dr. Gourde, and then Suzan admonished him for giving a resident such a menial task to perform. Yasiv was straining so hard to hear their voices that he didn't notice the footsteps approaching and was startled when a young man suddenly turned the corner.

Realizing that this must be the resident that Beckett was ordering around, he quickly fell into stride beside him.

"I'm sorry, I didn't mean to eavesdrop, but was that Dr. Campbell I overheard?"

The man, who looked in his early to mid-twenties with a shaved head and narrow nose, eyed him curiously for a moment.

Yasiv put on his best fake smile and held out his hand.

"My name's Henry Budaj, and I'm a grateful patient... well, not exactly a patient—that was my father. He had this tumor removed, and it was sent to Dr. Campbell... I think. Sorry, I'm not a doctor. Anyways, the results came back, and my dad is cancer-free now. I tried to send flowers to his house, but they just got returned. Something about no one being there to sign for them?"

The man continued to stare.

"Dr. Campbell is in his office now if you would like to go speak to him."

Yasiv shook his head.

"No, I don't have the flowers and, I mean, I don't want to go see him without bearing gifts. And before you ask, I don't need his address—I know you wouldn't be able to give me that, anyway—I just wanted to make sure that he was home now, so I could get them re-sent. And I guess you answered that question."

"Yeah, Dr. Campbell just returned from South Carolina a few days ago. But to be honest, I'm not sure he's a fan of flowers. Alcohol might be a better if you ask me."

Yasiv's eyes widened.

"Yeah? Thanks. I appreciate that. Any idea what his favorite drink is?"

"Scotch. I don't really know what kind, though; I don't drink much myself."

Yasiv beamed.

"Great—scotch it is. Thank you so much, young man. What's your name by the way?"

"Grant. Grant McEwing."

Up until this point, Yasiv had done what he thought was an admirable job portraying the family member of a grateful patient. But this... this threw him for a loop.

Yasiv was familiar with the McEwing family—they had donated the funds for the newly minted Transplant Wing of the Hospital.

And Flo-Ann McEwing, a sister or cousin to Grant, he surmised, had been murdered a couple of months back.

The murder had been attributed to another doctor, a Dr. Stransky, who had shortly thereafter taken his own life.

Another coincidence? Or another link between Beckett and his circle of death?

"I have to go now, there's something I need to do," Grant said, clearly growing uncomfortable.

Yasiv offered the man another smile, this one considerably weaker than the first.

"Yes, of course, and thank you again. You really have been very, very helpful."

Chapter 25

THE SECOND THAT BECKETT got home, he went down into the basement. Part of him still expected to find the body as he'd left it before his trip to South Carolina.

But it wasn't there.

Slightly disappointed, Beckett went to the spot where he'd seen the dot of blood and got on all fours, looking for more. None was visible to the naked eye.

With a sigh, he looked up and noticed that the boxes at the back of the room usually reserved for old textbooks had been moved—the center box was in front of the others, instead of in line with it. Curious, he rose and walked over to it.

Inside, he saw his projector as well as the shitty laptop that he'd used to show Wayne Cravat the video of him finding Bentley Thomas's body.

Did I put this back?

Beckett couldn't remember but didn't think so. He was about to push the box back into place when he noticed something buried at the bottom: a hard, plastic case about the size of a cigar box. After shifting the other items around, he pulled it out and then started to smile.

"Luminol."

Beckett recalled ordering the kit after watching a CSI episode years ago, back when they were still good, but had never opened it.

Excited now, he switched off the basement light and then, armed with the spray bottle full of Luminol in one hand and the black light in the other, moved to the center of the room.

Spraying conservatively at first, Beckett concentrated on the area that he'd found the dried blood. But when he illuminated the area with black light, his heart sank.

The concrete didn't light up.

"The fucking body was here," he grumbled.

Beckett sprayed more liberally now, nearly soaking the ground at his feet.

Still nothing, save a few spots that might even be false positives.

Placing his hands on his hips, Beckett looked skyward.

"How the hell did—"

His gaze fell on the stairs. Wayne Cravat's body had been sitting on top of a plastic sheet; if someone had taken his corpse out of the basement, the easiest way to do so without making a mess was to wrap it in this sheet and drag it upstairs.

Beckett made a 'humph' sound and walked to the bottom step and sprayed it with luminol.

It didn't light up, but he wasn't done yet; Beckett sprayed the next step, then the one after that.

The first hit was on the fourth stair from the bottom: a thin line of blue light illuminated the otherwise dark basement. Encouraged, Beckett continued to work his way upward. The trail disappeared at times, but before he knew it, he was back in the kitchen, and moments after that, he was standing in front of the back door.

Would you look at that? I'm not insane; somebody took the body out of the basement and out the back door.

Beckett paused to stretch his back as he looked through the window and into his backyard. It wasn't much, mostly patio stones and about a square foot of lawn, but there was also an eight by eight-foot shed that had come with the house.

He swallowed hard.

The shed... what if Wayne's body is in the shed?

No, he scolded himself. *Don't jump to conclusions. Follow the trail.*

Being late afternoon, it was still fairly bright out, and Beckett quickly looked around for something to block out the sunlight. The best he could come up with was a large black umbrella.

This might work, he thought as he opened it and then stepped through the door.

It took a little while to develop a quasi-successful approach. He settled on curling on his side so that the umbrella covered his entire body and blocked out most of the ambient light. It was difficult to spray the luminol and use the black light with his elbows pressed to his chest like a T-Rex, but he somehow managed.

And it worked... kind of.

Beckett found that if he pressed his nose against the patio stones, he could pick up the faintest trace of illumination. He continued this way, inching his way along on his side like an arthritic potato bug, for what felt like an hour. In the end, the trail led him right to the front of the shed.

Well, you could have saved yourself a lot of trouble if you'd just—

"Beckett? Is that you under there? What in God's name are you doing?"

PART III

Unexpected Visitors

Chapter 26

THERE WAS NO MENTION of Beckett, of a pathologist, or anyone else who fit his description, but Sergeant Yasiv was positive that the man was involved somehow.

The headline to the article that he pulled was simple, yet effective: *Police on the hunt for the Reverend who claimed to cure death.*

It went on to outline the atrocities perpetrated by the Reverend, including chaining the terminally ill in the basement of his parish until they passed. After the serendipitous discovery of the corpse of a woman afflicted with cystic fibrosis, the police started searching for Reverend Alister Cameron and his wife, Holly.

Three days later, they were still searching for them.

Yasiv had the sneaking suspicion that they wouldn't be found, not alive anyway. Not after Dr. Beckett Campbell had dealt with them.

Convinced now more than ever about the dark side hidden deep in Dr. Campbell's soul, Yasiv set about printing out images of all of the man's potential victims and pasting them on the whiteboard in his office. The first to go up was Craig Sloan, the only man that Beckett had actually admitted to killing.

The next was Bob Bumacher, followed by Winston Trent and then Alister and Holly Cameron. Finally, he stuck a photograph of Wayne Cravat on the board. Pleased with his work, Yasiv finished it off by adding the photo of Beckett from his University ID and drew red lines with a dry erase marker from him to all the others.

As he stepped back and stared at the board, Yasiv came to realize that every single one of the doctor's victims had something in common: they were all bad people. *Really* bad. Every single one of them had committed murder. Except for Wayne Cravat, of course. And if it hadn't been for that man, Yasiv might—*might*—have been able to do exactly as Detective Bob Crumley had suggested and just let it all go.

But Wayne was innocent; Wayne was a victim.

"He made a mistake in killing him," Yasiv said out loud. "A big mistake."

"Killing who?" a booming voice asked from behind him.

The sound was so startling that the dry erase marker slipped from Yasiv's hand and dropped to the floor.

Chapter 27

"WHAT ARE YOU DOING, Beckett?"

Beckett peeled his face away from the patio stones.

"Lost a contact," he replied instinctively. Realizing that his voice was muffled by the umbrella that he still held to block out the light, he threw it to one side and repeated his answer.

"I didn't know you wore contacts."

"I don't."

Beckett squinted and realized that the man speaking to him, and also peering over his fence, was Detective Dunbar.

His expression soured.

"I'm getting a lawyer," Beckett shouted. "I'm hiring F. Lee Bailey—this is harassment. Your boss already searched my house and all he found was my lacy underwear."

Detective Dunbar raised his hands to show that they were empty.

"No, no, I don't have a search warrant. I come in peace, man. I just wanted to talk to you, is all."

"Yeah, well, I'm not really in the mood for a conversation. Either you Mirandize and arrest me, or just get the fuck off my property."

Beckett had always had a good rapport with Detective Dunbar and even considered the man a friend, but he'd felt the same way about Henry Yasiv up until a few days ago.

"Beckett, I really need to talk to you."

"I'm a pathologist, not a psychologist. Go on, scat."

The man lowered his head and started to turn. But for some reason, Beckett felt a pang of guilt.

Fuck, maybe Dr. Swansea is right, maybe I am getting soft.

Despite these feelings, Beckett resisted the urge to call Dunbar back. Friend or foe, he had no time for the police right now.

"Alright, Beckett, you win," the man said as he walked away. "But I just wanted to let you know that I resigned today. I resigned because of what Hank is doing to you, because of this witch hunt. And I really just wanted to talk."

***

"I'd offer you a beer, but I'm fresh out. Scotch?"

"Yeah, sure," Dunbar replied.

Beckett was skeptical of the man's motives, which was why he'd set his phone to record and leaned it up against a bottle of wine on the counter. If any of this conversation did end up making its way back to Yasiv, at least he'd have a record of it.

He knew that he should've probably let the detective walk away, should've just focused on searching the shed, but if Wayne was in there... what would another hour matter? It would be worth it if he could tease out of Dunbar exactly what Yasiv had on him.

Oh, and a drink might calm his nerves, which was something that he desperately needed.

Beckett walked to the bar and poured them both a glass of scotch, opting for the cheap shit. Shit that would make the late Ron Stransky proud.

"Here," Beckett said, sliding the glass to Dunbar and taking a seat just out of frame of his cell phone video. "Now, as you know, I am a busy, busy man. So, what do you want to talk about?"

"There's something wrong with Hank," Dunbar began. His eyes remained on his drink as he spoke, which was unnerving.

"Yeah, he's a backstabbing cocksucker, but what else is new?"

Dunbar didn't even bat an eye.

"No, he's changed, Beckett. He's on some sort of crusade." Dunbar finally raised his gaze. "For some reason, he's focused on you—he's obsessed."

"Ya think?"

"No, you don't get it, he's gone off the rails. I mean, he's told every detective in the precinct that you're some sort of murderer. They're working around the clock, trying to dig up dirt on you. It's crazy, man. There are more people working on your case now, looking for evidence, than there was for Craig Sloan or the Download Killer. I've never seen anything like it."

Beckett's heart started to pitter-patter in his chest.

This was what he feared, the absolute worst-case scenario.

Because with his first kills, Beckett had been sloppy. Come to think about it, none of them had been perfect. Wayne Cravat had been the closest thing to a clean kill until his corpse went missing. There *was* evidence out there linking him to the crimes, and if what Dunbar said was true, it might only be a matter of time before Yasiv returned to pay him another visit.

A vision suddenly flashed in Beckett's mind. A vision of him with a scalpel pressed to Yasiv's throat before slitting it from ear to ear.

His fingers started to tingle, and he shook his head violently from side to side to try to make it all stop.

You can't kill him... you can't kill him. He's done nothing wrong. Yasiv isn't like the others, he isn't a murderer.

"You okay, Beckett?"

"Headaches... all this shit is giving me terrible headaches. I don't know what crawled up Yasiv's ass and laid eggs, but I'm going to lose my job over this. I'm a respected doctor—" Beckett rocked his head from side to side, "—correction, I'm a doctor, hard stop. An ME. But after what happened with Craig Sloan, I'm not sure the tribunal is going to give me a second chance." Beckett still wasn't sure if Dunbar was a friend or a foe in all of this, but he had to try to leverage the man as best he could. "Dunbar... I have no idea why Yasiv is out for blood, but I can't work like this. Is there... is there any way you can talk him down, get him to ease up? See the light and all that shit? Maybe the man just needs to get laid."

Dunbar sighed and sipped his scotch.

"I resigned—I mean, I tried to get him to back off, but he refused to listen. I told you, he's obsessed. I don't—fuck, I—" the man swallowed hard. "I gotta ask you something."

Ah, here it comes. I'm surprised it took this long. Everyone needs to hear the bray from the horse's mouth.

In preparation for the question he knew was coming, Beckett stood and made his way to the counter. With his back to Dunbar, he picked up his cell and stopped the recording.

"Beckett," Dunbar's face twisted. It was clear that this was the true purpose of the man's visit, and it made him incredibly uncomfortable. But you had to give him props just for showing up. "Did you—did you have anything to do with Wayne Cravat's disappearance? I mean, I don't know why or how, but did you—like, did you—"

Beckett turned around then, his eyes narrowing to slits.

"Yeah, as a matter of fact, I did. I killed him. I drugged the bastard, put him in my basement, and then slit his fucking throat."

Chapter 28

"DISTRICT ATTORNEY MARK TRUMBO, did we have an appointment?" Sergeant Yasiv asked after he'd collected himself.

The district attorney of New York County was a mountain of a man, with blond hair and thick jowls. He was clean-shaven and sported a navy suit and matching tie that extended past his belt buckle. Yasiv had had only a handful of interactions with the man and while all had been pleasant, they'd also been... *suggestive*. Their most recent encounter had been a personal visit, much like this one, when the DA had impressed upon Yasiv how important it was to find Wayne Cravat after the man had skipped bail.

Something told him that this visit, however, might be a little different.

"Do I need an appointment?" Mark asked, raising an eyebrow.

This comment was intentional, Yasiv knew, and it set the tone for the rest of the 'meeting.' It was no secret that while Mark had avoided the messy fallout after the mayor had been indicted, he was desperate to keep his job. Some had even suggested that he would make a run for the vacant mayor position.

"Just wondering if I missed something on my calendar. What can I do for you?"

"First off, you can tell me what murderer you were mumbling about as I came through the door."

Yasiv huffed.

"I was just talking to myself. Nothing to—"

The man silenced him by shaking his head.

"You were talking about a particular medical examiner for the state of New York," Mark answered for him. Yasiv intended to protest, but the DA held up a hand, once again stemming his words. "Sergeant, I suggest you rethink your recent course of actions. We just indicted the mayor of New York and he promptly fled the country. We don't need another fiasco like that one, especially if it involves another employee of the State."

As he spoke, the DA's gaze drifted to the board that contained the images of Beckett's victims that Yasiv had just completed. Yasiv debated turning it around, but the DA had already gotten an eyeful. Instead, he rolled with it.

"We have connected Doctor Campbell to five bodies, plus Wayne Cravat, whom you insisted that I go to great lengths to locate. All I need is—"

"Things have changed, Sergeant. Wayne Cravat is no longer a person of interest. As for Doctor Campbell... well, it's best if we just let him be."

Yasiv had patience for politics. He wasn't particularly interested in the sport, and he only had a rudimentary knowledge of the rules, but he knew firsthand the power of the game. What he didn't have patience for, however, was someone telling him how to do his job. No matter who that person was, or what political clout they held.

"I have nothing personal against Doctor Campbell. In fact, up until serving a recent search warrant, we had a friendly relationship. I'm just following the trail of evidence, that's all."

The DA pressed his lips together.

"A trail of evidence that is leading nowhere."

"I can't say I agree. And now that I have all my detectives on the case, I'm certain that my suspicions will be borne out."

"Hmph. Well, you *had* all your detectives on the case—but that's about to end. Either you pull them off, or I will. I want you to drop this, Sergeant Yasiv. I want you to drop this *immediately.*"

Yasiv shook his head.

"I really don't think that's a good idea. I mean, if Doctor Campbell really did kill these people as I suspect, then it's only a matter of time before he strikes again."

The DA frowned, his jowls lowering to his throat.

"Nope—not gonna happen. And don't go thinking that I'm the only one against this idea; I've heard that one of your detectives has already resigned over this.... *case.*"

Yasiv's eyes darted to the desk drawer that contained Dunbar's badge and gun.

How the hell does he know that? How can he possibly know that Dunbar resigned?

But it was a rhetorical question; There was only one way, of course.

There was a leak in his department.

Yasiv sighed and held his hands out, palms up.

"I'm just trying to do what you asked. You wanted Wayne Cravat found and Doctor Campbell will lead us to him."

When the DA spoke next, his tone had softened a little.

"Look, Sergeant, I appreciate your work with the Brent Hopper case, I really do. But, as I've already stated, our priorities have changed. I'm getting pressure from above and I don't think I need to remind you that the DA is an elected position."

The man's words hung in the air for several seconds.

Pressure from above?

With a vacant mayor position, the DA was top dog... or so Yasiv had thought.

Before he could come up with an appropriate response that wouldn't cost him his job, the DA stood and buttoned his suit jacket.

"Drop it, Yasiv. For both our sakes."

With that, the man turned and left the room, leaving Yasiv to stew alone.

Drop it?

It was this sort of pressure that had allowed Mayor Ken Smith to rise to power. It was this sort of back-scratching bullshit that had poisoned the city that Yasiv loved.

You know what? I don't think I will drop it, Trumbo. Not for the Senior Medical Examiner of New York State and definitely not for a district attorney who likely only has a few months left before he's unemployed.

Instead, I think I'll push even harder.

Yasiv might be naïve when it came to the world of politics, but the one thing he did know for certain, was that when someone insisted that you leave an issue alone it wasn't because you were barking up the wrong tree.

It was because shaking this tree would cause a whole lot of nuts to fall out. Nuts that had the potential to land on people's heads, to end their careers.

To put people behind bars.

Which was exactly where Dr. Beckett Campbell belonged.

Chapter 29

DUNBAR GASPED.

"You... you *what?*"

Beckett laughed.

"You really believed me? I'm fucking with you, Dunbar. Jesus, my reputation really does proceed me. I didn't kill anybody, don't be ridiculous. I'm a doctor, for Christ's sake," he held his arms out, showing off his tattoos. "Sure, I may not be your typical MD, but I *am* a doctor. I took the Hypocritical Oath or whatever the hell it's called. Jesus..."

Dunbar closed his mouth, but it didn't appear as if he was completely convinced. Not just yet, anyway.

"But... but do you remember when you called me about the driver's licenses and the organ donor stickers?"

"Of course. And we both know how that played out. Doctor Ron Stransky was the one responsible for murdering those people and sending those organs to me—God only knows why. Twisted bastard. Shit, the poor girl who was murdered?"

Beckett pictured Flo-Ann McEwing as she lay on her kill table, telling him that he was just like her.

No, no I'm not like you.

"Well, her brother, Grant McEwing, is one of my residents, for Christ's sake. I had nothing to do with that like I had nothing to do with Wayne what's-his-name's disappearance. Hell, I've been doing my best here to keep my nose clean after... well, after you know who."

Dunbar nodded.

"Craig Sloan."

Beckett shrugged.

"Look, I'm not gonna lie and say that I feel bad for the guy. Craig Sloan was a piece of work, a murderer, and he tried to kill my girlfriend. I'm not sorry for what happened to him. I guess people like Yasiv want me to say, aw, shucks, I wish we had a proper trial for the misunderstood medical student." Beckett performed a mock fist pump. "What a shame, he could be saved, reha-ha-habilitated. Yeah, well, I'm more likely to stick my dick in a meat grinder than do that. You *know* me, Dunbar; I'm honest, I'm straightforward. I don't play games and don't believe in euphemisms. This rubs a lot of people the wrong way, especially the old guard who are used to doing things all prim and proper-like. But that just ain't me."

Dunbar took another sip of his scotch, and the tension seemed to release from his shoulders.

Finally.

Beckett decided to lighten the mood a little.

"You really resigned because of me?"

Dunbar nodded, his eyes again locked on the scotch.

"Well, I'm touched—that sort of thing fills my heart with love. I really appreciate you coming here, talking to me, letting me know about Yasiv. I have no idea what happened to Wayne Cravat, and honestly? I don't rightly care. Like Craig Sloan, he was a piece of shit. But, look, I've got stuff I need to do—lost my contact, that sort of thing."

Dunbar finished his scotch and rose to his feet.

"I wish I could do more to help you."

Beckett nodded. Dunbar was in a hard place, but he'd taken a stance, done what he believed was right. They had that in common, at least.

"You've done enough. I appreciate it."

They shook hands and Beckett led Dunbar to the door. The detective turned back twice on his way across the street, his mouth partly open, but didn't say a word on either occasion. In the end, he just got in his car and left.

Beckett stood in the doorway of his home trying to wrap his mind around what the detective had told him when his gaze drifted across the street.

"You've got to be shitting me," he grumbled.

A black Lincoln Town car was parked just a couple of houses down. Beckett feinted closing the door, pretending not to notice the vehicle, then bolted from his house.

The car immediately roared to life and the driver slammed it into reverse. But he was too slow.

Beckett hammered on the hood with both hands.

"What the hell do you want from me?"

He tried to see the driver through the windshield, but it was too darkly tinted to make out anything but shadows.

"What the hell—"

Beckett tried to strike the hood again, but the car picked up speed and he could no longer keep pace. Instead of pounding on metal, his palms smashed into the asphalt, sending searing pain up to his elbows.

"Just leave me alone!" he screamed as the car continued to accelerate. "Leave me the fuck alone!"

Chapter 30

SERGEANT YASIV SAT IN his office contemplating the DA's words, or threats, long after the man left. The thing was, Trumbo's job was to decide whether or not to press charges. But, as sergeant, it was Yasiv's duty to allocate resources to where he saw fit.

Eventually, his wandering eyes fell on Beckett's photograph on the whiteboard.

I'm coming for you, Beckett, and I won't give up. My team won't either.

With that, the sergeant of 62nd precinct got to his feet and walked over to the conference room. There were three detectives inside, all hunched over their computers.

The rest were on the street and at old crime scenes, trying to dig up something concrete on Beckett, something that not even the DA would be able to overlook.

Let it go, Yasiv... the order came from above.

Yasiv opened the door to the conference room and stepped inside.

Who the hell was above the DA?

"Sergeant?" Detective Gabba asked as he entered the room. One of the old guard, the hefty man in his late fifties could be counted on for obeying the chain of command.

"You guys still working on the Campbell case?"

All three detectives exchanged glances.

"Yeah... why? Has there been a change?"

Yasiv shook his head.

"No. No change at all. What've you got for me?"

Detective Gabba's eyes flicked to his laptop.

"So far I haven't found anything aside from a cocaine charge that was thrown out more than ten years ago. Want me to dig deeper into that?"

Yasiv frowned; Beckett wasn't involved in drugs, not seriously, anyway. He knew that doctors who worked hard sometimes liked to play hard, occasionally with the aid of pharmaceuticals, but that wasn't of interest to Yasiv. Besides, if he was right, Beckett had taken out a major heroin trafficker in Bob Bumacher.

"No, don't bother. What I want you to do is look into Dr. Campbell's most recent vacation to South Carolina. See if there's any connection between him and Reverend... Reverend..." Yasiv racked his brain for the man's name, but it eluded him.

"Do you mean Reverend Cameron? The crazy guy who was keeping sick people trapped in his basement? That Reverend?" Detective Gabba offered.

Yasiv raised an eyebrow.

"Yeah," he replied hesitantly. "*That* Reverend."

Clearly, sensing his apprehension, Detective Gabba felt the need to explain.

"Yeah, I heard about that guy—a real piece of work. Took off once the heat was on and hasn't been seen or heard from since. You think Dr. Campbell had something to do with those people trapped in the basement? All that weird genetic testing stuff?"

Yasiv thought about this before answering. Based on what he knew about Beckett and his preferred victims—murderers, mostly—he didn't think so. By all accounts, the Reverend preyed on innocent people who were unfortunate enough to not only suffer from rare diseases but to also be the target of the man's sick game. What was more likely, he concluded, was that Beckett was involved in the Reverend and his wife's disappearance.

Yet, Yasiv was hesitant to reveal too much information to these detectives, given that he'd already established that there was a leak in his precinct.

"I dunno, maybe," he said at last. "The Reverend was performing some crazy medical experiments, so who knows. Just look into it."

Yasiv was about to leave the men to their task when Detective Gabba called him back.

"Sergeant? What about the DA?"

Yasiv chewed the inside of his cheek and chose his words wisely.

"What about him? He just wanted to touch base on some things. Don't worry about that, you just keep looking into Dr. Campbell."

Without giving the man an opportunity to reply, Yasiv left the conference room. He debated going back to his office, but he'd already done everything he could there. Besides, he knew that it was only a matter of time before the DA caught word that he hadn't given up on Dr. Campbell and decide to pay him another visit. Perhaps it was better if he was unreachable, at least for the foreseeable future.

But he couldn't hide forever; he had to find irrefutable evidence that Beckett was involved in at least one of the murders. Something that the man couldn't pass off as just lazy or careless ME work, as in Bob Bumacher's case.

This line of thinking made Yasiv consider what Beckett did in his spare time, what he liked to do for fun.

Or, what he did on vacation.

So, he kills Wayne Cravat, then goes off to South Carolina with his girlfriend?

Yasiv's eyes narrowed as he made his way toward the front of the station and started to pull a cigarette out of his pack.

Vacation... vacation... vacation...

A smile crept onto his lips.

Beckett had taken another vacation recently, one that hadn't been so... *voluntary*.

After it had been 'suggested' that he take some time off following the Craig Sloan incident, the doctor had spent a week or two in Virgin Gorda.

And it just so happened that somebody Yasiv knew well had met up with Beckett on the exclusive island.

After lighting up, Yasiv crossed the parking lot with a spring in his step and got into his car. Then he made his way across the city to DSLH Investigations... or Triple D... or whatever the hell Damien Drake's Private Investigation firm was called now to meet up with Stephen 'Screech' Thompson.

Chapter 31

BECKETT CURSED A FEW more times and then slowly walked back to his house. Several of the neighbors were peeking through their windows at him, but whenever he tried to catch them in the act, lights turned off, and blinds snapped closed.

Fuck them, he thought. *Fuck them all.*

He didn't care what other people thought of him, provided those people weren't in the NYPD and couldn't put him in prison for life.

Scowling, Beckett rinsed the dirt out of the cuts on his palms and then hurried into the backyard. He kicked the umbrella to one side and then stood in front of the shed with his hands on his hips.

The padlock on the door appeared locked, which was problematic; he could never remember where he put his car keys, let alone the keys to a shed that he rarely used. He considered calling Suzan to ask her where the keys were but decided against it. In his present state, the conversation would likely go like this:

Beckett: Hon, I'm just wondering where the keys to the shed are.

Suzan: Oh, thinking about doing some gardening? Planting some kale, perhaps?

Beckett: No, no; kale is for hipsters and women with incontinence.

Suzan: Then why do you need to get into the shed?

Beckett: Well, you see, I think somebody took the corpse of the man I killed out of the basement while we were in South Carolina and jammed him in the shed, that's why. Now, do you know where the keys are, or not?

On a whim, he reached out and grabbed the lock. To his surprise, while the padlock was closed, it wasn't fully locked.

"I've got you now, Wayne," Beckett whispered as he removed the lock and then slid the door open triumphantly.

His heart sank.

"Damn."

The shed was empty, save a handful of seldom-used lawn tools and a bucket of white paint.

Frustrated, Beckett was about to slam the shed closed when he noticed that the wooden floor was slightly darker near the center. Leaning down, he swiped two fingers across the surface, and they came back wet. Not with blood, mind you, but with what appeared to be water. A quick glance upward revealed that the roof was still in good shape and that there were no signs of water damage anywhere.

Beckett retreated to the yard to collect the luminol and blacklight and then proceed to spray the wet area on the floor of the shed. He paused, then thought, *what the hell*, and soaked the entire shed with the magical fluid.

He waited for thirty seconds, then turned on the blacklight, thankful that the shed was dark inside, and he didn't need to fiddle with the umbrella again.

"Wow."

Beckett suddenly felt like he'd dropped a hit of acid; either that or Copernicus was wrong, and his shed was actually the center of the universe.

Nearly every square inch of the wooden walls and floor was peppered with glowing stars.

Beckett shook his head.

"Okay, Wayne, that's one mystery solved. You *were* here."

He was in awe of just how much blood there was in the shed. It looked as if he'd killed Wayne here, with a blunt instrument, instead of in his basement with a scalpel. Maybe even tossed the fat man in a blender without the top for good measure.

"You *were* here, but now you're not. So, where the fuck did you go?"

There were only two options, so far as Beckett could ascertain: one, somebody had moved the body from the basement to the shed, but then found out about the search warrant and proceeded to move the corpse to a secondary location; or, two, Wayne was undead.

"Where the hell are you?"

And then, as if the cosmos were replying to his query, his cell phone buzzed.

Without thinking, Beckett answered immediately.

"Wayne? That you?"

"What? Who's Wayne?"

He shook his head.

"Nothing—nobody. Who's this?"

"Dr. Campbell, it's Grant."

"Yeah?" Beckett replied, his eyes bouncing from one glowing star to another.

"So, I looked into the doctor that you asked me about? A Dr. Gourde?"

The man had Beckett's full attention now.

"And? Did you find anything?"

There was a short pause, and then Grant cleared his throat.

"Anything? Oh, I found a bunch. Dr. Campbell, I think it's best if I show you this in person, back at your office. Can you come in? Like, now?"

Chapter 32

THE FIRST THING YASIV noticed was that the *D* in *DSLH Investigations* had been scraped off the frosted glass door. This surprised him; after all, even though Drake wasn't in the country, he was very much a part of the team. In fact, he was their figurehead, their curmudgeonly leader, the person who had started the PI firm after being let go from 62nd precinct.

But that wasn't his concern now. Yasiv rapped his knuckles off the glass inlay and waited. The door opened, and a pretty woman with dark hair tucked behind her ears peered out. She had a small scar on the underside of her chin that was only visible because of the way she held her head: high and proud.

"Hey, Hanna, how are you? It's been a while."

"It has... looking for some more pro bono PI work, Sergeant Yasiv?" she replied with a grin. When Yasiv's expression didn't change, Hanna stopped smiling. "And that would be a yes." She opened the door all the way and stepped to one side. "Sure, why not; after all this place runs on unicorns and lollipops. Come on in."

Yasiv had been here once before, but he was again startled by the drastic change in surroundings. Triple D Investigations—the first iteration—had been a dive, while DSLH—or SLH—Investigations was pristine, sterile, and professional.

He wasn't sure he liked it. Drake, Yasiv knew, would hate it.

Seated behind one of the desks was a man in his mid-to-late twenties, with short blond hair and a neatly trimmed goatee. Screech looked up as Yasiv entered and offered a weak smile.

"Sergeant Yasiv, I'm hoping that you come bearing good news about Drake—about him being allowed back into the country without being arrested."

Knowing that there was no answer that would satisfy the man, Yasiv instead focused on a large painting hanging from one of the walls. A red dot had been painted in the center of a white canvas, with several smaller ones making a semi-circle around it.

"Nice painting," he remarked.

"Thanks, I'm partial to it, too," Hanna replied as she took a seat on Screech's desk.

Despite working together to bring in Stephanie Loomis, and put an end to ANGUIS Holdings, things were still strained between Yasiv and the rest of Drake's crew. Screech was convinced that Drake should be given a pardon for his 'transgressions' based on all the good work he'd done for the NYPD. But while Yasiv tended to agree, it was out of his hands; he'd spent countless hours trying to convince the officer who pressed charges against the former detective to drop it, but the man hadn't budged.

To both Officer Kramer and DA Trumbo, Drake was just another crooked cop who needed to be punished like all the rest.

"That's a no, I'm guessing," Screech said with a frown, bringing Yasiv back to the present.

"Unfortunately not. I'm still working on it, but as of yet, there's nothing I can do. The warrant for Drake's arrest still stands. The good news is that when a new mayor is elected, he's going to want to hire his own DA. I'm hoping that when a new district attorney takes the post, he'll toss Drake's case out—start with a clean slate, so to speak. Even if he doesn't, I'll petition hard, just like I'm doing now with the current DA.

I can't promise anything, but I'm hopeful that things will change, that he'll be able to come back to the US soon."

All this was true, of course, except Yasiv neglected to mention the part about the current DA's desire to become the next mayor. If that happened, things would become considerably more complicated for Damien Drake.

Screech made a disappointed *hmm* sound, then said, "I hope you're bringing us some business then because things have been pretty tight around here since the last time we spoke."

"I thought business would've picked up after you got Mrs. Armatridge's charges dropped."

"That was Beckett, not me. And yeah, for a while things were good, but the unfortunate thing about old people is, they tend to die. And this place is expensive. What we really need is a celebrity to come in, an athlete with deep pockets maybe, who is willing to pay big to solve their problems. That's what we need."

"Well, I'm no athlete, but I'm a mean cribbage player. Speaking of Beckett…"

It was a strange segue, but as Yasiv let his sentence trail off, he let his eyes drift to the door leading to the only private room in the office.

Screech shook his head.

"We're a team here; this isn't Drake running the show anymore, it's us. Me, Hanna, and Leroy. Whatever you want to say to me, you can say in front of them."

Yasiv looked over at Hanna, who was feigning being bashful.

The woman was a bit of an enigma, someone who he didn't know much about. Yasiv knew Leroy, about the kid's struggles growing up and how he got involved with Drake following his brother's murder. He was also aware of Hanna's role in Drake's escape from the psychiatric institution, and before that, how she'd lied about being raped by the man they all thought was the Download Killer. But everything before that was a mystery.

Yasiv made a mental note to take a deeper dive into Hanna after this whole Beckett thing was cleared up.

Beckett thing... that's what you consider this? Mass murder has just become a thing to you, Hank?

He shook his head.

"How are those PI licenses I got you working out? They still okay? Still valid?"

Screech's frown deepened, letting Yasiv know that his not-so-subtle reminder of the favor did not go unnoticed.

Nor was it intended to.

"What is it that you want, Sergeant Yasiv?"

Sergeant Yasiv, not Hank, Yasiv noted. *All right, two can play this game. We don't have to be friends. After all, friends of yours always seem to be getting into trouble with the law. And that's the last thing I need right now.*

"I'm going to get straight to the point, then. I need to ask you about your vacation in the Virgin Gorda."

Screech's eyes narrowed even further—they were but slits now.

"What about it?"

"We're trying to piece together a couple of things about the island that you stayed at, about the route that Bob Bumacher used to bring the girls over from Columbia. We know that he stopped offshore and moved the girls from the yacht to the shipping container, but we're focusing on the people who live on the island. If they knew what was going on, if they helped out in any way, that sort of thing."

"I'm no lawyer, but I think that's outside your jurisdiction, is it not?"

Yasiv cocked his head.

"It is, but if they ever made their way to the US..."

"Look, all I can tell you is that I found the yacht moored at the Virgin Gorda. As you know, I was hired by Bob Bumacher to find his yacht—that's it. At the time, I knew nothing about ANGUIS Holdings or the Columbian girls."

Yasiv held his hand up.

"I'm not accusing you of anything, just trying to get a lay of the land. Now, it's my understanding that Beckett was there with you? He's a personable guy... maybe he knows about the island people? Whether or not they were involved?"

Screech pressed his lips together so tightly that creases formed at the corners of his mouth.

He knows something, Yasiv thought suddenly. *He knows something.*

"Well, that's something you're going to have to ask Beckett."

"But you guys are friends, aren't you?"

Screech suddenly rose to his feet, and Yasiv instinctively knew what was coming next. A friendly, not-so-friendly walk to the door.

"This is you getting to the point? Seriously, what do you really want, Yasiv?"

Yasiv stuck to his story.

"Like I said, just trying to wrap up the ANGUIS file, tie up loose ends."

"I thought we did that already? I thought after Stephanie Loomis was put in jail and her father was... well, I thought that after all the high-ranking members of ANGUIS Holdings were out of the picture that this was all taken care of. Actually, now that I think about it, I'm pretty sure that *you* told me that."

And there it was; the in that Yasiv needed to veer just a little off course.

"Yeah, that was fucked up, wasn't it? Captain Loomis being shot and killed on his own estate like that. I'm glad, though, that we managed to work together to bring ANGUIS down. So, I know that Leroy was there," he nodded at Hanna, "as were the both of you. But what about Beckett? Was he there that night, too?"

Screech appeared at a loss for words, but Hanna quickly chimed in before things got awkward.

"Oh, suga', it was my debutante ball," she said in a comically thick southern accent. "I went solo."

Yasiv stared at her for a moment before shaking his head and turning back to Screech.

"He was there, wasn't he? Beckett, I mean. The reason I'm asking is because of Captain Loomis. There are some inconsistencies in the ME's report. Officially, the case is still open, but unofficially? It's been put on ice. But I still want to know what—"

Screech's face suddenly turned a deep shade of red and he took a large stride forward.

"Get out."

Yasiv was taken aback by the sudden change in the man's usually affable tone.

"I just want to—"

"Get out!"

Yasiv started backing toward the door.

"I didn't mean to upset you, I'm just—"

"Get out!" Screech screamed.

Yasiv reached for the door and pulled it open. Then he stepped into the hallway. But instead of just bowing his head and walking away, he turned to look back in SLH Investigations.

The anger...

He'd seen Screech angry before, but not like this. *Never* like this.

What the hell is going on here?

"Screech, I—" Yasiv stopped mid-sentence and decided it was now or never. "He killed him, didn't he? Beckett killed Captain Loomis—I know it. I know he did."

For a second, Screech's eyes went wide, then he grabbed the door and closed it so hard that it rattled on its hinges, and the frosted glass nearly exploded in Yasiv's face.

Chapter 33

"Okay, Grant, you're on the clock. What've you got?" Beckett asked, interlacing his fingers and leaning back in his chair, only to immediately sit back up again. The chair was so damn uncomfortable that it felt like a leftover relic from the Spanish Inquisition.

Grant, oblivious to Beckett's discomfort, stared down at the sheet of paper in his hand and started to read.

"Dr. Aaron Gourde, thirty-nine, got his medical degree from the University of Texas, then did his neurosurgical residency at Emory in Atlanta. He also completed a Ph.D. at the same time. After graduating, he was briefly married, but that was annulled after just a few weeks; I'm fairly certain that he's a homosexual. Likely just to get away from his ex-wife, Dr. Gourde moved out of Atlanta and took a position at the Cleveland Clinic. And that's when the strange things started to happen. He only spent six months there before being let go. Budget cuts were cited as the reason for his departure, but after digging deeper, I think it was related to a botched disk repair surgery on a—"

"Wait, wait a second," Beckett interrupted. "Dr. Gourde is gay?"

Grant made a face.

"That's what you're focusing on?" he shook his head. "Yeah, I think so. Anyway, after the Cleveland Clinic, Dr. Gourde moved on to Mass General, but less than a year after that, he was again let go when—"

"No, wait—wait a second. How do you know he's gay?"

Grant was clearly becoming frustrated now.

"Well, after his failed marriage I found his profile on Grindr. Now, please, Dr. Campbell, could we—"

"*You're* on Grindr? I mean, not that there's anything wrong with that. In college, I even—"

"Please! Dr. Campbell!"

Beckett unlaced his fingers and held up his scratched palms.

"Sorry, geez, you don't need to be ashamed of it. I'm not judging you. Go on, go on."

Grant rolled his eyes and took a deep breath.

"Okay, as I was saying, Dr. Gourde moved around a lot ever since graduating. The reason for his departure was always something vague like budget cuts. But he left a string of horribly botched surgeries in his wake. There are records of Dr. Gourde paralyzing people, leaving them in a coma, etc. But it wasn't until he set up his private practice here in New York that people started dying."

"*People?*" Beckett said, picturing Mr. Leacock's corpse lying on the gurney. "You mean there's been more than one victim?"

Grant nodded voraciously.

"Yeah—three. Three dead patients, but zero investigations or reprimands, outside of being let go. Probably with a glowing recommendation, but I'm still looking for proof of that. One thing's for sure, though; Dr. Gourde has no intention of stopping."

"Why the fuck do hospitals keep hiring this guy?"

"Well, he has his own practice, so..."

Beckett looked skyward.

"Before that, I mean."

"You mean when he became the Director of Surgery at Mass General?"

Beckett's eyes bulged.

"*Director?* What the fuck?"

"Yeah, best I can figure it, nobody at the previous hospitals reported anything about Dr. Gourde's past performance, and the new hospitals didn't look into him as they should have."

Beckett scoffed.

"Come on, what hospital would hire a doctor without first looking into their past?"

Grant's eyes not so-subtly drifted to the tattoos on Beckett's arms, and he subconsciously folded his hands on his lap.

Well played, Grant. Well played. But let's not forget that you got into residency without ever actually getting a medical degree. Ye who judgeth...

"What do you think? You think that Dr. Gourde is doing this on purpose? Or is he just the worst fucking surgeon ever?"

Grant was about to speak when Beckett waved his response away preemptively.

"Naw, don't answer that. There's only one way to find out."

Beckett locked eyes with his resident.

"What? Why are you looking at me like that?"

Beckett continued to stare until Grant suddenly caught on and the man shook his head.

"No, I don't think so. I don't think that's a—"

"Grant, you need to do this. For the people."

Grant sighed, and his shoulders slumped.

"That's the spirit." Beckett rose to his feet and clapped the man on the back. "Let me know how the consult goes."

With that, he guided Grant out of his office. Just before the man walked away, however, Beckett asked a final question.

"Hey, Grant, are you *sure* that Dr. Gourde is gay? Like *really* sure?"

Chapter 34

YASIV LEFT SLH INVESTIGATIONS more confident than ever that Beckett was a murderer. And now, he was also certain that Captain Loomis had been one of the doctor's victims.

Back in his office, Yasiv printed out a picture of the Captain and added it to the board with the others. He was in the process of drawing a line to Beckett's face when Detective Gabba burst in.

"You're not gonna believe this," the man said excitedly, holding a laptop in his arms.

"Believe what?"

"I found it... what you asked for."

It was almost as if the man was surprised that he'd been given a task and had actually completed it. Under normal circumstances, Yasiv would have been concerned by this, but the entire case had transcended normal a long time ago.

"Show me."

The detective turned the computer around and clicked play.

"I found a video of Dr. Campbell at Reverend Cameron's parish. Not only that but—"

"Shh," Yasiv hushed him as he tried to focus on the laptop. At first, all he saw was a crowd of people, but eventually, the camera zoomed in on two in particular: Reverend Cameron and Dr. Beckett Campbell.

By the time the video was over, Yasiv's jaw was on the floor.

"Play it again," he said dryly.

"I know, it's fucked up. Weird—"

"Just play it again!"

Detective Gabba did as he was asked, but the video didn't become any less amazing the second time around. In it, Yasiv saw Beckett on his knees with the Reverend hovering over him. With more than two dozen parishioners gathered around, the man of the cloth reached out and touched Beckett's forehead. Instantly, the doctor's eyes rolled back, and he started to tremble. Reverend Cameron's fingers tensed, and then Beckett began speaking in tongues. Although it was a convincing show, it was clear that Beckett was just mocking the man.

Up until the last few seconds of video, that is.

All of a sudden, Beckett's jaw clenched, and his lids started to droop. Then he collapsed in a heap on the church floor.

"Any idea what he's saying?" Yasiv asked after several silent moments.

Gabba shrugged.

"No idea. Mostly nonsense with a few choice words sprinkled in."

"Play it once more, would you?"

Gabba nodded and clicked play. This time, however, nothing happened.

"That's weird."

The detective spun the laptop around and started to attack his keyboard.

"What's wrong?"

"I dunno... the video's gone—says that it's been taken down."

"What? What do you mean?"

"Yeah, says here that it's been flagged for... what the fuck? *Inappropriate gender pronouns?*"

Yasiv squeezed his eyes closed.

What in God's name is happening?

"Can you get it back?" he asked.

"I'm not sure. I can try."

"Alright, you do that, and while you're at it, try to find more links between the Reverend and Dr. Campbell."

Detective Gabba looked up at him then, a question on his tongue.

"What? What is it?"

The detective took a deep breath.

"Well, it's just that there are some rumors going around about the DA wanting to pull the plug on this whole thing? I just want to make sure that everything is—"

Yasiv felt his ears grow hot.

The fucking leak... the goddamn leak in my department.

"Detective Gabba, last time I checked, *I'm* the sergeant of the 62nd precinct. Also, the last time I checked, *you* work for *me*. So, why don't you focus on doing your goddamn job and let me deal with the DA? Okay?"

Chapter 35

BECKETT ALMOST MADE IT out of the pathology department free and clear. He would've, if it had been Delores at the front desk, and not the annoying temp.

"Dr. Campbell?" the temp asked as he approached.

He cringed.

"Yes?"

Still not even bothering to look up from her computer, the woman said, "Dr. Hollenbeck is looking for you. He said it's urgent."

Beckett glanced at the department head's office, the door of which was slightly ajar.

"Is he in his office?" Beckett practically whispered.

The temp was about to answer when a gravelly voice spoke from behind him.

"Dr. Campbell, could you please come into my office."

Beckett whipped around to look at Dr. Hollenbeck. The man was at least a hundred and fifty years old, with hair that looked like a long-abandoned bird's nest, eyes like white marbles, and a thin line for a mouth. It was the Crypt Keeper in the flesh, minus the maniacal laugh.

Fuck, just what I need.

"Dr. Campbell?" the man repeated, his eyes darting about. The words sounded curiously like a question and not a request.

I don't have time for this. I've got to get ready for dinner with Suzan, I have to check on Delores, I have to find Wayne's body, I have to follow up with Dr. Nordmeyer...

This last part gave him an idea.

"Actually, I'm Dr. Nordmeyer," Beckett said cheerily. "Dr. Campbell is in the morgue right now."

Oh, please tell me the man didn't get his cataracts fixed yet...

Dr. Hollenbeck frowned.

"You're... you're Dr. Nordmeyer?"

There was a hint of a question in there, so Beckett decided to run with it.

"Yeah, of course, I'm Dr. Nordmeyer. But I understand how you could be confused. To be honest, Dr. Campbell and I look a lot alike."

The man grunted then looked at the secretary for confirmation.

"Delores?"

Beckett couldn't help but grin. Dr. Hollenbeck was blind as a bat.

"No, that's just a temp. Delores took a few days off. I said it was all right."

Despite this claim, it appeared as if the elderly pathologist needed support and continued to stare, rather awkwardly, at the temp. She opened her mouth to say something, but Beckett quickly pulled out his wallet and wagged it in her direction.

"You're just a temp, right?" Beckett reaffirmed. "And I am Dr. Nordmeyer."

The secretary looked at the wallet and then at Dr. Hollenbeck.

Eventually, she shrugged.

"Yep. Just a temp. It's my first day."

Apparently satisfied now, Dr. Hollenbeck turned to Beckett and nodded.

"Okay, Dr. Nordmeyer. Do me a favor, and if you see Dr. Campbell, can you please tell him to join me in my office? There is something important that I need to speak to him about."

Beckett was tempted to ask what this was all about but resisted pushing the envelope. He was almost free.

"Yes, of course. I'll be sure to do that. *Toodles.*"

And then, like a scared jackrabbit, Beckett bolted from the department and drove home. His intention had been to make Suzan dinner as he'd promised, but he suddenly didn't feel like eating in. The image of someone dragging Wayne's bloated corpse up the stairs then through the kitchen was enough to make his stomach lurch. Instead, Beckett decided to treat his extremely patient girlfriend. After all, she deserved it for putting up with his shit. And Beckett knew just the place, a restaurant that Suzan had been dying to try out ever since she'd read about it in *Gourmet* years ago. It would take calling in a few favors, and didn't have chicken and waffles, but still...

***

"I thought you were making us dinner, Beckett? You know, you and me, alone at home? That sort of thing?" Suzan asked as the maître d' led them to a table with a clear view of the window.

"Yeah, but—"

"—but this is... well, it's great. How in the hell did you manage to get reservations at *Dorsia's* on a Friday night?"

"Well, I'm not just anybody, you know," Beckett replied, with a smile.

"Here you are, Dr. Halberstram," the maître d' said as he pulled Suzan's chair out for her. She sat, then the man repeated the process for Beckett's seat as well.

It was a hundred times more comfortable than the one in his office.

The maître d' let them know that he would be back shortly with the specials, and then left them alone to talk.

"Dr. Halberstram?" Suzan asked, eyebrow lifted.

Beckett shrugged.

"Role-playing—keeping it fresh and all that. Know what you want?"

Suzan's eyes dropped to the menu in her hand.

"I haven't even looked yet."

"I heard the sea urchin ceviche is to die for," Beckett offered.

Suzan scanned the menu for a moment, before looking up at him again.

"I don't see that on here."

"Darn, they must've changed it since the eighties."

Suzan stared at him for several seconds before saying, "What? The eighties? You're even stranger than usual tonight. What gives, Beckett?"

Well, to be honest, after killing Reverend Cameron and his wife, I'm itching to add another notch in my belt... or tattoo on my side, as it were. Just looking for the perfect victim. Speaking of which, did you happen to notice a body in my basement recently? May or may not have also been in my shed?

"It's this Delores thing. Messing with my head. Making me rethink my mortality and all that."

"Yeah, that's terrible. Did Grant find out anything about the doctor?"

The sommelier came by with a wine list, but Beckett blanket accepted his first suggestion.

"Yeah, Dr. Pumpkin is gay."

"Okay, *riiiight*. But did he find out anything pertinent? Anything about the man's surgical prowess, by chance?"

"Oh, yeah—he's terrible. Grant told me that he's killed at least three people and has worked in three different hospitals since graduating. And now he runs his own private clinic here in New York. It seems that no matter how bad he is as a neurosurgeon, the man just keeps getting shuffled around."

Suzan looked appalled.

"Really? That's terrible."

"I know! I make a *correct* diagnosis, reverse a mistake that Dr. Nordmeyer made—which I may or may not have contributed to in the first place—and I get hunted by the police. This guy kills people and gets hired as the Director of Surgery. It's absolute nonsense."

The sommelier returned with a bottle of wine and showed it to Beckett. He nodded and then the man poured a smidgen into his glass. With Suzan watching on, Beckett made a show of the tasting, putting his pinky finger high in the air and swirling the liquid so dramatically that it almost spilled out of his glass. He finished this charade by gargling the wine obnoxiously.

"Orgasmic," he gasped. The now frowning sommelier quickly filled their glasses before departing.

"You always have to make a scene, don't you, Beckett? Or should I say, Dr. Halberstram?"

Beckett chuckled and sipped his wine. It was delicious, which made him think that he should have checked the price of the bottle before ordering. No matter how expensive it was, however, if he kept annoying Suzan this way, he'd end up in the doghouse. Or maybe the shed...

"Listen, Suze, I've just got a quick question for you: have you been in my shed recently? Asking for a friend..."

Chapter 36

"DETECTIVE BRADLEY, THIS IS Sergeant Henry Yasiv from the 62nd precinct of the NYPD. Do you have a moment to chat?"

"Just finishing up my dinner. What's this about, sergeant?"

Yasiv stared at the yellow legal pad in front of him and tapped the man's name. Detective Boone Bradley was the fourth one on the list; the first three had lines through them. There was only one name after Detective Bradley's.

"I can call back if this is a bad time," Yasiv offered, praying that the man would say differently.

"No, it's all right. Like I said, just finishing up. What can I do you for?"

"Well, to be honest, I'm calling about a case, about the—"

"The Reverend Cameron case," the detective finished for him. "Figured. Who did you say this was again?"

"Sergeant Henry Yasiv from the NYPD, 62nd precinct. Badge number 80443." Yasiv paused, hoping that the man would use this time to confirm his information. "I understand if you're reluctant to talk about the case, given the media shitstorm surrounding it. But I was hoping that maybe we could help each other out."

"Hmm. Go on." The man was guarded, but at least he hadn't hung up on Yasiv like the others.

"Well, we've had some similar crimes here in New York, and I think they might be linked. No hard evidence yet, nothing worthy of getting the FBI involved, but enough to warrant a chat. Informally, of course."

There was a longer silence this time.

When Detective Bradley finally spoke, he sounded surprised.

"You've had similar crimes to Reverend Cameron and his wife's in New York?"

Shit.

"No, no," Yasiv said quickly. "Well, not exactly. What I meant was that I think that Reverend Cameron might be connected with a crime syndicate here in New York."

"How so?"

There were optimism and hope in the man's voice, and Yasiv decided to go for broke.

"I'm guessing you heard what happened in New York... how the mayor was the head of a drug-smuggling ring?"

"I think everyone in the nation heard about that. You think that Reverend Cameron was involved somehow?"

Now it was Yasiv's turn to hesitate.

"I don't want to overstep, but the reality is that we have a bunch of cops, and the mayor himself, who fled the country to avoid indictment. I heard that Reverend Cameron and his wife might have done the same."

"Yeah, that's the way it looks. Mrs. Cameron's purse was missing, as well as their passports. Their cars are still here, and we don't have no record of credit card transactions since the last day they were seen. But they had money... the church raised a lotta money in the weeks leading up to their disappearance. We've got BOLOs out, but I don't know if we'll ever see them again. Sergeant... can you be more specific here? I'm having a hard time seeing how this has anything to do with your problems up in New York."

"I can't get into the details over the phone..."

"Alright, well, I don't see how we can possibly help each other out then. Have a nice—"

"Wait!" Yasiv blurted. "I agree... I don't think you'll ever see the Reverend and his wife again... not alive, that is."

Detective Bradley's voice seemed to kick up an octave. "And why do you say that?"

"Because... because they're dead. What I'm hearing up here in New York, Detective Bradley, is that both Reverend Cameron and his wife were murdered."

Chapter 37

"YOUR SHED? WHY WOULD I go into your shed?" Suzan replied instantly.

Beckett shrugged.

"I had some rare blood diamonds in there, but they've gone missing. The lock was open, and I wasn't sure if... naw, never mind. Not a big deal. Did you decide on what to order?"

Suzan was evidently getting used to this new, nonsensical Beckett because she didn't even bat an eye.

"I think I'll go for nice T-bone. You?"

"I could do pasta. Carb up for later," he said with a wink.

They chatted idly while they ate, talking mostly about Suzan's classes, including her most recent test and how she'd aced it. That was good; with all the shit that was going on in their lives, including their botched vacation, the cops hounding them, and Delores's father's death, Beckett thought that her work might suffer. But, as usual, Suzan proved once again that she wasn't just a wallflower, that she was strong.

Her father's murder had done that to her, Beckett supposed, and then everything that had happened since had only strengthened her resolve and character.

Beckett found himself staring at Suzan a lot during the meal, at her pretty face, the way she spoke and didn't seem to care who was listening. Suzan Cuthbert was something special, and not just because she managed to put up with him.

Eventually, however, their conversation circled back to Trevor or Taylor or whatever man bun's name was and how he'd taken a nose dive back at the body farm.

"I swear, that was an accident, Suze."

"Sure," she said with an eye-roll. "I'm just pissed that you didn't take me there. That place... I've heard stories. It's supposed to be creepy, gross, and utterly fantastic."

Beckett grinned.

"Yeah, it's something. Pretty damn gruesome. I know you're not squeamish, but my residents? One of them puked more than Angelina Jolie after an all-you-can-eat buffet at the Waffle House."

"Beckett..."

As if on cue, their food finally arrived. Suzan tried not to make a face when a giant medium-rare T-bone was slid in front of her, but Beckett caught her flinch.

"Seriously, I'd like to go some time."

She hesitantly cut a piece of meat, but he noticed that she didn't put it in her mouth. Not yet.

"Alright, sure. I know the guy who runs the joint. I can get you in." Beckett pointed at his chest with his fork. "Got the hookups."

"Okay, P-Diddy."

Suzan brought the piece of meat to her mouth, then pulled back at the last second.

Beckett smiled.

"What's wrong? Lost your appe—you little motherfucker!"

"*What?*"

Beckett didn't even hear her. His eyes were focused on the window, on the black Lincoln Town car that had just pulled up and flicked off its lights.

Yasiv's goons were back. Beckett felt a little like Eminem being asked for an autograph while taking a shit.

"Beckett? What's going on?" Suzan asked, craning her neck around to follow his gaze.

"Give me a fucking break," he hissed from between clenched teeth.

Beckett rose to his feet so quickly that his knees struck the underside of the table, rattling their plates and cutlery. This drew the attention of those around them—*Dorsia's* was as pretentious as they came—but he didn't care.

Without a word to Suzan, he strode toward the door.

"Beckett? *Beckett!*"

The maître d' looked at him as he passed, but he must have seen the fury in Beckett's eyes because the man didn't even question the fact that he hadn't paid their substantial bill. Keeping his head low as he exited the restaurant, Beckett initially turned in the opposite direction of the parked car.

His hands were still raw from their last encounter, but this time, he wasn't going to let these bastards get away without a fight.

The car suddenly roared to life, and Beckett swore, realizing that he'd been made. He turned and ran like a madman toward the vehicle. Seconds before he made it to within striking distance, the driver flicked his high beams on and Beckett cried out.

It was as if this Lincoln model had lights powered by plutonium. They were absolutely blinding, and Beckett was forced to stop his forward advance and bring his arm up to shield his eyes.

And then something struck him in the side, and he immediately recoiled.

"Fuck!"

The car pulled away and Beckett blinked rapidly to clear his vision. Eventually, he managed to focus on what had hit him.

It was just a woman walking her child.

"Shit, sorry," he said, realizing that it was he who must have bumped into her, and not the other way around.

"What's your problem?" the woman in the pea-coat demanded.

Beckett took a step back.

"I'm sorry, I didn't mean to. I was blinded and—"

"Beckett!"

He turned around in time to see Suzan leaving from the restaurant with her jacket on and her purse slung over her shoulder.

"Suzan? What—I'm—I'm sorry it's just Yasiv's guys are following me everywhere. I can't fucking stand it."

Suzan glared at him.

"I'm going home. Ordered an Uber. Get your act together, Beckett. There's something wrong with you."

I won't argue about that.

Beckett turned back to the woman and child one last time.

"Ma'am, I'm really sorry about that. I didn't mean to bump into you."

"Just watch where you're going next time," she said, tugging on her daughter's arm. "Or I'll pepper spray your ass."

Good ol' New York. God, I hate you sometimes.

"Sure, have a great night!"

Beckett hurried back to Suzan, but she was already halfway in her Uber.

"I'm sorry," he pleaded. "I—I—do you even have your keys?"

"Don't need them. I'm staying at my mother's place tonight. Looks like you could use a little break. Some alone time."

"Suzan, *please*. I'm sorry."

Suzan's reply came in the form of slamming the Uber's door, leaving him alone on the curb with his proverbial dick in his hand.

I know I'm acting weird, but what about you?

Suzan was due for one of these types of explosions—she was a woman, after all—but the situation didn't warrant her storming off like this, did it?

Sometimes Beckett forgot that she was only in her early twenties.

When will she grow up and act like... well, like a real adult and not so much like me?

Beckett swore and started back to the restaurant when he realized that a half-dozen people had stopped in the street to look at him.

He threw his hands in the air.

"Who wants a selfie with a recently castrated man? You? You? How about *you*?"

PART IV

Old and New Wounds

Chapter 38

PREDICTABLY, BECKETT DIDN'T SLEEP well that night. It wasn't just the fact that his headache had returned, along with the accompanying tingling in his fingers, but also that, once again, he'd managed to fuck things up with Suzan.

So, he just lay there, in his boxers, among the faces of his victims etched in the glow of moonlight. Partway through the night, he rose and tattooed two new lines on his ribs: one for the reverend, and one for his wife. Beckett briefly debated adding a third to represent C.J. Vogel, the poor soul who had suffered immensely at the hands of the Reverend but decided against it.

That wasn't *his* kill; that was an act of mercy from which he had derived zero pleasure.

Satisfied with his work—his lines were becoming straighter and more precise—Beckett placed a small strip of gauze over the new tattoos.

Sometime later, when Beckett's consciousness had drifted into the ether that occupied the space between sleep and wakefulness, headlights filtering in through the window vanquished his shadowy demons.

Even in his transient state, he knew exactly which car those lights belonged to, and he snapped fully awake.

His first instinct was to retrieve the black leather case from his side table, the one that contained his pre-loaded syringes and a fresh scalpel.

"You can't," he whispered. And yet, despite realizing that his words rang true—the black case was reserved for the Reverend Camerons of the world—Beckett's eyes remained locked on the drawer for the better part of a minute.

The headlights finally flicked off, knocking him out of his trance. Beckett quickly left the bedroom and found a more appropriate tool in the front closet: a Louisville Slugger that still had that 'new bat' smell.

Then, clad only in his boxers, he gripped it tightly in both hands. He enjoyed the way the wood felt on his palms, despite opening up a half-dozen tiny cuts that hadn't healed yet since his last encounter with the men in blue... and soon to be black.

Black and blue... I don't care if they are NYPD detectives or police officers, this is the last time they're gonna be setting up shop outside my house.

Without turning on the lights, Beckett crept downstairs and made his way through the kitchen to the front door. Then he unlocked the deadbolt and waited in the dark.

Glancing through the peephole, he spotted the black Lincoln parked across the street and two houses down. Beckett figured it would take him fifteen seconds, maybe a little longer with the baseball bat in his hands, to open the door and run to the car. Because the car was off, he estimated that if the driver wasn't snoozing or distracted, it would take him at least five seconds to start the engine, and another five or six to put it in gear.

Close enough, he thought. *Close enough.*

After a deep breath, Beckett gripped the bat halfway down its length and then threw the door wide.

He'd been wrong; it took him only eight seconds to reach the car, even though the ground was hard and sharp on his bare feet. And the driver *had* been distracted. By the time the baseball bat was in motion—an Aaron Judge-worthy majestic arc—the car roared to life.

"Get out!" he screamed just as the bat struck the window.

The glass didn't smash inward as he expected, however; it bounced off with such fervor that it sent Beckett flying backward.

"Get out!"

He righted himself and planted his feet before swinging for the fences once more. This time, the window stood no chance.

It exploded inward, raining the interior of the Lincoln with shatterproof cubes.

Beckett had expected to see the shocked faces of police officers inside, in uniform or even in plain clothes, but what he hadn't been expecting was to be confronted by two young men in tuxedos.

"What the fuck?"

The driver took advantage of his confusion and put the car into gear. But Beckett recovered in time and jabbed the end of the bat through the window, lining it up with the side of the man's head.

"I said, get out!"

The driver leaned away from him, covering his face with his arms and hands.

"Stop, please, stop," he pleaded.

Beckett looked at the passenger.

"Who are you guys?" he demanded.

When neither man answered, Beckett jabbed the bat into the forearm of the man behind the wheel.

"Fuck, just take it," the passenger replied. For the first time, Beckett realized that the man was holding something out to him, something white and rectangular.

A small envelope, perhaps.

Beckett's eyes narrowed.

"Who are you? Did Yasiv send you? Because I don't give a—"

Before he could finish the sentence, the passenger flicked the envelope at him. He might've looked like a frat boy, but, evidently, the man was also some sort of secret ninja. The envelope flew out the window like a ninja star and struck Beckett directly in his left eye.

He blinked just before impact, avoiding any serious damage, but it was still so jarring that he was forced to back up and instinctively doubled over.

The driver seized this opportunity and the Lincoln rocketed forward, nearly running over Beckett's toes in the process.

With one eye closed, Beckett screamed—mostly in frustration—and swung the bat wildly at the gravel that shot from the rear tires and pelted his bare chest.

Then he swore again, this time at the top of his lungs.

A light switched on in the house directly across from him, and Beckett realized that it would be in his best interest not to stand in the middle of the street looking like a drunken pirate swinging his peg leg around.

Before going inside, however, he made sure to bend down and pick up the white square that had hit him in the eye.

It was indeed an envelope, a small four-by-two-inch rectangle that had cursive writing on the front.

With his injured eye still squeezed tightly, he had to bring it close to his face to read the words. Thankfully, he was intimately familiar with them.

"Dr. Beckett Campbell," he read out loud.

Well, he thought, as he hurried back to the open door of his house. *At least they spelled my goddamn name right, whoever these ass-clowns are.*

Chapter 39

FOR THE PAST FEW weeks, Sergeant Yasiv had made a habit of sleeping in his office. Not every night, mind you, but it didn't make sense to make the hour drive home when he was working late. And with the recent developments in Dr. Campbell's case, he wasn't just working late but well into the night.

Which was why, when he got a text from Detective Bradley, who was under great pressure to find the Reverend and his wife, he was still wide awake.

And as soon as Yasiv received the message, he immediately dialed the man's number.

"Sergeant Yasiv?" Detective Bradley said in his Southern drawl. "Didn't expect you to call so soon. Melting the midnight grease, are you?"

"Yeah, something like that. So, you found blood at the reverend's house? How much?"

The detective paused.

"I looked you up, you know."

Yasiv closed his eyes, his frustration compounded by the lack of sleep. He didn't want to talk about himself, or anything for that matter, that wasn't directly related to Dr. Beckett Campbell.

"Yeah?"

"Seems you're legit. Seems like you brought down the mayor and that corrupt army guy... what's his name?"

"Captain Loomis."

"Yeah, that's it."

In the ensuing silence, Yasiv struggled over what to say next. *Was this a test? Is he testing me?*

Yasiv sighed.

"Yeah, I looked you up, too," he lied. "As I said earlier, I really think we can help each other."

"Uh-huh, you said that, sure, but I'm still having a hard time figuring out what your angle is in all of this."

"I don't have an angle," Yasiv began, then quickly changed tactics. He couldn't afford for Detective Bradley to brush him off. "But, here's the thing, we busted up this elaborate sex trafficking ring related to the corruption scandal a while back. One of the names of the girls that popped up on our end was an alleged victim of Reverend Cameron." He cringed, ashamed of the lie. "We're just trying to wrap everything up, you know?"

"Yeah, I hear you; the media vultures are intense down here, so I can only imagine what they're like in New York. Anyway, we did find blood in the Reverend's house, quite a bit of it, actually. Someone did a pretty good job of cleaning up, but they always leave a trace. Not gonna be able to do any of that fancy DNA stuff on it, but it's more than enough PC to take a closer look."

What? The torture and kidnapping of critically ill women weren't enough to 'take a closer look'?

"Good, that's good."

"Yep, got the cadaver dogs ordered. Gonna be here in the mornin'."

Another pause, which gave Yasiv a moment to think. Unfortunately, he knew how these things worked. When a convicted, or sometimes even a suspected killer went missing, or worse, killed, nobody wanted to put in the time or resources to bring their murderer to justice.

With Craig Sloan, everyone had been more than eager to chalk the incident up to self-defense; in fact, the DA had basically leaped at the opportunity to avoid taking such a case.

The media would have been, as Detective Bradley had just remarked, intense, and the public outcry would have matched or exceeded it.

Even if they find the Reverend and his wife's body, how hard is Detective Bradley going to look for their killer? Would he just let the case run cold?

Yasiv pinched the bridge of his nose, remembering the man's words from moments ago.

He needed blood evidence to 'take a closer look'. What do you think, Hank?

"Well, okay, Sergeant, thanks again for reaching out, and if we find anything related to that girl there, I'll, uhh—"

"How you doing for manpower down there, Detective?" Yasiv interrupted.

Men like Mark Trumbo and Detective Boone Bradley, and even Drake or Chase, might be able to overlook certain cases based on the pedigree of the victim, but Yasiv couldn't.

He couldn't, because of men like Wayne Cravat.

Because of the innocent people who got caught in the crossfire.

"What? What do you mean? I've got—"

"Could you use one more hand? Because it's getting mighty cold here in New York and I could do with a little bit of that Southern sun… if you have enough to spare, of course."

Chapter 40

BECKETT HAD NO SOONER made his way into his kitchen when he heard another sound, this time coming from the back of his house.

"Here we go again," he mumbled, tossing the envelope onto the counter and hurrying toward the back door. He opened it just in time to see a figure all in black exit the shed and then start to climb over the fence.

"Hey!" he cried, taking a step outside. But the figure didn't turn or even acknowledge him. Instead, they just fell awkwardly into the alley that ran behind his house. Beckett heard a grunt, then they were gone.

He was too tired to chase after the person, and his eye hurt like hell. It didn't matter, anyway; it wasn't as if there was a body in his shed.

With a heavy sigh, Beckett headed back inside. After making sure to lock the back door, he reluctantly returned his attention to the mysterious envelope.

"If this is some Publisher's Clearing House bullshit, they really need to work on their marketing," he said, as he turned the envelope over in his hands.

In addition to his name on the front, the back was sealed with some sort of dark wax.

"The fuck is this?"

Holding it up to the light, Beckett could see three letters pushed into the seal: *D N R*.

With a frown, he tore the seal off and then opened the envelope, hoping to find a check with many zeros inside.

He was disappointed.

In place of a check, there was a small card, only slightly larger than a business card. Black on one side, and white on the other. No, not white, but *bone*. And the text was written in Silian Rail font.

Saturday.
Midnight.
Black-tie.
2155 Hastings Rd.

His frown became a scowl.

Beckett flipped the card over to the black side and saw his name written in white text.

For several seconds, he just stared at the card, wondering if it was the most elegant, and obscure, ransom note ever devised. Then he crumpled it up and tossed it in the garbage.

I always hated blind dates," he whispered. After gingerly probing his sore eyelid, Beckett wondered if he should ice the wound and then drop a few cubes into a tall glass of scotch.

Naw, only a plebian puts ice in scotch.

Chapter 41

SERGEANT HENRY YASIV TOUCHED down in Charleston, South Carolina at seven-fifteen a.m. He hadn't slept at all the night before and was running on a steady diet of caffeine and nicotine.

Even though he'd claimed that it was cool in New York, that had been a lie; it was unseasonably warm, touching in the low eighties some afternoons. But South Carolina? That was a different beast altogether. Even at this early hour, the sun was hot and oppressive. Within five minutes of leaving the airport in a taxi, heading to the address that Detective Bradley had given him over the phone, the sweat stain on the back of Yasiv's white button-down resembled the horn of Africa.

He arrived at the police station, paid the driver, then smoked furiously before heading inside. His outfit drew many curious glances, but nobody approached him.

Annoyed, and knowing that he had to act quickly before the DA caught wind of where he'd gone, Yasiv grabbed the closest officer—a man who looked as if he'd graduated yesterday—and gave his name.

"Detective Bradley... you know him?"

The man raised a blond eyebrow.

"He's hard to miss."

Yasiv didn't know what to make of this but continued anyway.

"Yeah, well, he's expecting me."

The officer gave him a once over, his eyes lingering on the multitude of sweat stains.

"What did you say your name was, again?"

"Sergeant Henry Yasiv. From New York."

The man's eyes lit up.

"Ah, yes. Come on, I'll take you to him. My name's Officer Oliphant, by the way."

"Nice to meet you; so Detective Bradley's here?"

"He was—he's always the first one here. But now he's over at the Reverend's house."

Yasiv's heart sank, thinking that he was going to miss out on whatever the cadaver dogs might discover. Officer Oliphant must have seen something in his face because he smiled and quickly added, "Don't worry, don't worry. Detective Bradley said he'd wait for you until eight. Which means we gotta hurry, but we still got time. Things move a little slower down here in the South."

***

Detective Boone Bradley was nothing like how Yasiv pictured him over the phone. For some reason, he'd always imagined Southern Carolina detectives as being lean and hard; like New York detectives, only more tanned and not as gray.

But Detective Boone Bradley was anything but hard. In fact, the only thing even remotely hard about him was his expression. Yasiv figured the man topped the scales at least three-hundred pounds. As a result, he moved slowly, but with purpose. And, while Yasiv was undeniably sweaty as he hurried up to the Cameron house, Detective Bradley looked as if he'd just stepped out of the shallow end of a pool.

"Really appreciate you letting me come out here," Yasiv said, extending his hand. A slimy, uncomfortable handshake ensued.

"Not a problem," Bradley said. "Sorry I didn't meet you at the station, but the cadaver dogs were already on the scene." The man raised an arm and indicated an SUV with a large blue stripe that read 'K-9 Unit' on the side. Standing in front of the vehicle was a thin black man wearing white Oakley's. In each hand, he held the leash of one of the apparent cadaver dogs.

Even the animals looked to be uncomfortable in the heat, their pink tongues hanging out of their mouths.

Wanting to get down to business, Yasiv hooked a chin at the large house behind the detective.

"Is that the Cameron residence?" he asked.

"Yep. I'll take you inside and show you where we found the blood."

"Sounds good."

The detective languidly made his way up the front steps, but before entering the house, he turned back to the man in the Oakley's. He gave a simple flick of his wrist and the handler nodded. The man then leaned down, scratched each dog behind the ears, and unhooked their leashes.

Unlike Detective Bradley, they took off like a shot toward the back of the house.

"The house was in perfect order," Detective Bradley informed Yasiv as they finally stepped inside. "Which was partly why we suspected that Reverend Cameron and his wife simply left."

The man continued to ramble on, but Yasiv ignored him. He was focusing on the interior of the house, imagining how things went down in here.

In his mind, he could see the Reverend tied up in a chair, perhaps begging for his life. Maybe the man's wife was in the chair across from him, her face streaked with tears.

Beckett probably made the Reverend watch his wife die, Yasiv thought. *He probably—*

"Sergeant Yasiv, you all right?" Detective Bradley suddenly asked.

Yasiv shook his head and stood up straight.

"Yeah, fine. Just not used to this heat."

"You've been staring at the place where we found the pool of blood for a couple of minutes now," the detective informed him.

Yasiv blinked. There was nothing on the floor that suggested there had once been blood there; it looked exactly like the rest of the surrounding hardwood.

That's strange...

"You sure you're okay?" Detective Bradley asked again, his wide face etched with concern.

Yasiv rolled his neck and wiped sweat from his brow.

"I'm fine."

He was about to add more when the man in the Oakley's peered through the open door.

"Dogs hit on something in the back. Y'all wanna take a look?"

Yasiv pulled a cigarette out and put it to his lips.

"Yeah, we do. We *definitely* wanna take a look."

Chapter 42

BECKETT MADE HIS WAY through the underbelly of NYU Med, somehow managing to avoid speaking or even acknowledging any of the other dead-eyed doctors prowling the halls.

He was tired, his head hurt, and he was more confused than ever.

But Beckett still had work to do; not only had he made a promise to Delores that he would investigate what happened to her father, but he also needed to find Wayne Cravat.

He just hoped that Dr. Nordmeyer wasn't there to slow him down.

As usual, if Beckett didn't have bad luck, he'd have none at all.

Dr. Karen Nordmeyer was huddled over the nude body of a woman who appeared to have been shot in the head. There were two other bodies on adjacent gurneys awaiting inspection, as well.

Three bodies, one pathologist. If only there were a second forensic pathologist, perhaps even a Senior Medical Examiner, who could help offset some of the workload.

It was clear that whoever was pulling the strings, was using said threads to divert work *away* from Beckett.

His university position was safe—thank God for tenure—and while he enjoyed torturing his residents, he missed his work as an ME.

Well, lucky for you, assholes, I'm not going anywhere... unless I can't find Wayne Cravat's bloated corpse, that is. Then I'll be going away for twenty-five to life.

"Karen," he said as he approached the woman. She startled and then collected herself and turned. The thick rubber gloves that ran to her elbows were coated in blood, as was the Sawzall gripped in her right hand. On the gurney, Beckett saw that the woman's chest cavity had already been opened wide, and her ribs cut clean through.

Even from behind the ridiculous, oversized plastic face-shield that nearly reached her clavicle, Beckett could see Dr. Nordmeyer's face droop when she realized that it was him.

"I'm busy," she said in a voice that was warbled by the plastic.

Beckett strode forward, suppressing a smile when Dr. Nordmeyer instinctively leaned away from him.

"I understand—just came for an update on Mr. Leacock."

Did her finger just tighten on the Sawzall trigger? Beckett wondered. *You know what, I think it did.*

"Then you're going to have to wait for the report to become public because I already submitted it to Mr. Trout and he's had it sealed."

Now it was Beckett's turn to be startled.

"Sealed? Why the hell did he do that? And why did you submit it to him without showing me first? I asked as a professional courtesy for—"

Dr. Nordmeyer stepped forward, lifting her mask as she moved. Then she 'accidentally' activated the Sawzall, speckling Beckett's jeans with dots of blood.

Oh, Suzan's gonna be pissed... you know how hard it is to get blood out of denim?

"Professional courtesy?" Karen mocked, her features pinching. "Really? *You—you* wanted *me* to show you some professional courtesy?"

Beckett held his hands out to his sides.

"Man, these walls echo more than I remember. But, hey, gimme a break; it's been a while since I've had a case down here."

"After what happened with Armand Armatridge, you, Dr. Campbell, Senior ME, want me to be courteous to you?"

Becket wasn't in the mood for this.

"No, no, I've got an idea; why don't you just get the fuck over yourself, already? You made a mistake, I made a mistake. Pot-*ay*-to, pot-*ah*-to. I fixed the mistake. Now, tell me what happened to Mr. Leacock, tell me how he died."

Karen glowered at him and raised the Sawzall a few inches.

Oh, for Christ's sake, put it down, Karen. We both know you aren't going to use it on me.

"I'm busy," she said, resorting to her previous refrain. She bobbed her head, which caused the plastic shield to fall back into place. Fed up now, Beckett reached out for her and gripped her bicep tightly.

"We're all busy. Life's fucking busy; you gotta breathe, eat, shit, get laid occasionally. Look, I know you went to Sergeant Yasiv with that shit about Bob Bumacher. Good, great — who knew that mollusks could grow spines? But, hey, I don't care. I just want to do right by Mr. Leacock."

Dr. Nordmeyer's eyes went wide.

"Do right by him? Like you did right by Bob Bumacher or Winston Trent? *That* kind of right?"

Beckett squeezed a little harder and stared into her eyes.

"You don't want to be on my bad side, Karen," he said in a flat voice.

Instead of backing down, she raised the Sawzall even higher.

"Let go of me," Dr. Nordmeyer demanded, trying to mimic his flat tone. She almost got it right, too; there was just a slight tremor to her voice.

But Beckett obliged, anyway. He smiled and held his hands up.

"Okay, okay, tough guy. I just want to know what happened to Mr. Leacock, that's all. Are you gonna tell me, or am I going to have to go visit Pete Trout myself?"

For a moment, it looked as if she might relent, but then Karen snarled.

"It's sealed, Dr. Campbell."

With that, she turned her back to him and started to cut the cadaver's ribs... ribs that had already been severed.

Holy smokes... I actually hired this feral cunt?

Beckett wanted to strangle her then, and if the sudden tingling in his fingers were an indication, he had the capacity to do it, as well.

If you're going to kill every woman that annoys you, Beckett, you're going to be exhausted before you leave Lululemon on 5th Avenue.

With a sigh, he headed toward the elevator. As the doors started to close, he leaned out and shouted over the whir of the saw, "Nice talking to you, Karen! Next time I see you, I hope you try to part your hair with that goddamn thing!"

Chapter 43

"MIGHT JUST BE A rabbit," Detective Bradley offered when he finally sauntered to the spot that the dogs had indicated.

Yasiv took one look at the area of freshly turned dirt and knew differently. It wasn't his place to say so, however, but, in the end, he didn't have to; the handler, Oakley man, said exactly what he was thinking.

"These dogs are trained to identify the odor of decaying human flesh, not small animals," he informed them as he scratched one of the dogs behind the ear. He pulled two treats from a fanny pack on his waist and held them out while he reattached their leashes. "Good boys, good boys!"

Detective Bradley just shrugged, which struck Yasiv as an odd gesture from a man who, just yesterday, was being lambasted by the media.

"What now?" Yasiv asked the other officers, all of whom just stood there, staring at the area that the dogs had indicated.

Detective Bradley turned to Officer Oliphant.

"Did you contact CSU?"

"Yep, just put the call in. They said they might be a while, though."

It took all Yasiv's willpower not to scoff.

A while? A fucking while? They've been waiting for a break like this and thanks to me, they get it... and now they're just going to stick their thumbs up their asses and wait? Well, fuck that.

Still shaking his head, Yasiv looked over at Detective Bradley.

"You guys have a shovel?"

***

Ten minutes into the dig, Yasiv followed the other two police officers' lead and removed his shirt. Now, close to two hours later, he regretted that decision; his pale flesh was bright red and sensitive to the touch.

When they uncovered the tarp, however, the pain instantly vanished.

"Two bodies," he said, pulling a cigarette out of his pocket.

Detective Bradley, who had literally done nothing but stand in the shade of the Cameron house and mouth-breathe since the dogs had hit, finally moved away from the building and peered inside the hole.

"Could be," he admitted, with a shrug.

Yasiv looked down at the dirt-covered tarp as he smoked. *Could be...?*

At roughly six feet long and half as wide, there was no question in his mind what was wrapped in the tarp: the bodies of Reverend Alister Cameron and his wife, Holly.

"Well, let's find out then, shall we?" Yasiv said, flicking his cigarette butt away and leaning toward the hole. When no one tried to stop him, he turned to one of the officers. "You guys have gloves? Evidence bags?"

The shirtless police officer who only went by the name 'Donald' looked to Detective Bradley, who nodded his approval.

Donald then turned to one of the uniformed onlookers.

"Go grab the kit."

This second officer turned and walked around to the front of the house. Although he was a third of the size of Detective Bradley, he somehow managed to walk even *slower* than the much larger man.

Yasiv found himself nearly continuously shaking his head in frustration. There were a lot of things not to like about New

York City—the taxi cabs, the traffic, the steaming sewer grates—but pace of life wasn't one of them. This was torture.

Eventually, however, the officer returned with 'the kit'. Yasiv practically tore it out of his hands, quickly donned a pair of gloves that were two sizes too big, then reached down and grabbed ahold of a corner of the tarp.

He took a deep breath and pulled.

Nothing happened.

Yasiv planted his feet and used both hands this time to pinch the tarp. Then he yanked—*hard*—but the tarp still held fast.

Wheezing now, he looked up at Donald and said, "Give me a hand, would you?"

Donald quickly sprang into action, making his way to Yasiv's side.

"On the count of three," Yasiv instructed, tightening his grip on the tarp. "One... two... *three!*"

Both men pulled at the same time and the tarp unfurled so quickly that they stumbled backward. Donald fell on his ass, but Yasiv somehow managed to stay on his feet.

Both men's eyes, however, remained locked on what they'd unearthed the entire time.

Then Donald gasped and Yasiv felt his stomach do a summersault.

Chapter 44

"**What do you mean,** *one day*?" Beckett barked into his phone. "You mean they did the x-ray, diagnosis, pre-op, and now they want you to go under the knife… all in the same day?"

"Yeah, that's what they said. But that's not the strangest thing about all this."

Beckett was no surgeon, but he was familiar with the typical surgical routine and patient management. Even in private practice, it usually took a week, minimum, from first seeing a patient to putting them under the knife for something like a degenerated disk. Even then, a week was an ultra-fast turnaround time that required the perfect coordination of everyone from the anesthesiologist to insurance providers.

"What could be stranger than that?" he asked.

Grant cleared his throat.

"Beckett, you're forgetting something…"

Beckett shook his head and wondered if Grant had already undergone the procedure, which had resulted in some sort of personality change.

"Yeah, I forget a lot of things. You see, I get these fucking headaches and I have a pain in the ass girlfriend. I'm also missing a finger, am usually constipated, and it's that time of the month for me. Just spit it out."

"Well, the weird thing is, Dr. Gourde wants to operate on my neck. But… but there's nothing wrong with my neck; there never has been. I told him that I had pain from an old football injury like you suggested as Delores's father had, but my neck is just fine. To be absolutely sure, I even had a buddy in the hospital take a look at my x-rays. Disks are healthy and fine.

"There's nothing wrong with my neck, Dr. Campbell, and yet I'm supposed to be going under the knife."

Beckett's eyebrows rose so high up his forehead that they threatened to join his hairline.

"Alright, alright, you win. That is *stranger*."

"No kidding. I mean, what happened to Mr. Leacock might have been an accident, but today's diagnosis? At best, Dr. Gourde is running an extremely dangerous insurance scam."

Beckett mulled over Doogie Howser's words for a minute.

There's something wrong with Dr. Pumpkinhead. Something very wrong with this man.

As if on cue, his fingertips started to tingle again.

"Dr. Campbell, you still there?"

"Yep."

"What do you want me to do now?"

"You know what, Grant, I want you to go through with the surgery."

Grant balked.

"There's no way. I mean, I'm all for helping you out and everything, you and Delores's father, and I think we're doing important work here, but I'm not going under the knife for—"

Beckett shook his head.

"No, no. I don't actually mean have the surgery, you dork. *Pretend* to have the surgery. Go back to the clinic, do all the pre-op stuff this afternoon and then I'll come in with my guns drawn and save the day. Catch this guy in the act, you know? What time is the surgery scheduled for?"

"Four-thirty. But I'm supposed to meet the team earlier, around three-thirty, to get some more imaging done. I go under at four. I have to say, though, I'm still not—"

"All right, I'll be there at two forty-five. Got something I need to do first, though."

"But, uhh, I don't know if, uhh, I just..."

"Don't worry, I'm *never* late, Grant. And thanks. I owe you one... not a medical degree, but something substantial. A nice bottle of wine, maybe."

Grant cleared his throat.

"I don't really drink that—"

Beckett hung up the phone before Grant could weasel his way out of this one.

Yep, there really is something wrong with this doctor. Who wants to bet that daddy gets a new tattoo soon?

***

The door to the office opened and a man huffed as he entered. When he switched on the light, he nearly jumped out of his skin.

"Dr. Campbell? What in blue blazes are you doing here?"

Beckett just stared and crossed his feet on the man's desk.

"Dr. Campbell?" There was serious concern on Peter Trout's face now, and he cautiously took a step backward.

"I guess I should have studied to be an Assistant HR whatchamacallit instead of spending more than a decade becoming a forensic pathologist. I mean," he pulled his feet off the desk and then squeezed the chair on either side of his hips. "Look at this thing? *Goddamn.* What's it made of? Alpaca foreskin?"

Peter Trout blinked and remained in the doorway. His keys were still dangling from his fingers, and there were a briefcase and folder wedged between his arm and body.

"Is there something I can help you with, Dr. Campbell?" he asked at last when it was clear that Beckett wasn't going anywhere.

"Yes, actually. Believe it or not, I think you can help me." Beckett stood, and Peter's Adam's apple bobbed.

"Ok, *umm*, do you want to make an appointment, then?" Beckett laughed. He couldn't help it.

"Appointment," he repeated, shaking his head. "Yeah, sure. Listen, bud, I need to know the results of Mr. Leacock's autopsy."

Peter looked relieved and constipated at the same time. It was quite the combination.

"I'm sorry, but I can't reveal anything about that case. It has been sealed."

Beckett frowned and stepped forward. Instead of being intimidated, however, the man held his ground. He even puffed up his chest a little.

My god, what is with these people?

"Yeah, I heard about that. I also heard from a little birdie that you guys had a tribunal about it just a few hours ago. What's the rush, Pete?"

The man averted his eyes.

"I'm not at liberty to discuss cases — open or sealed. I'm sorry, Dr. Campbell, but if you want to know about the results of the case, you can put in a formal request. I will caution you, however, that it is highly unlikely that any information that was discussed at the tribunal will be released to you, or anyone else. There are severe legal implications, and — "

Beckett's hand shot out and he grabbed the man by the collar.

"I would love to open you up and see what makes you tick," he growled.

"Wh — wh — what?" Peter Trout stammered, fear returning to his face.

"I said, *I am aware of the legal and insurance implications of releasing the results of a potentially damning legal case as they pertain to both the hospital and the private clinic in which the surgery was performed.* But I want you to know that Dr. Pumpkinhead killed my friend's father. That's just... that's just not right, Pete."

Peter had to shift to make sure that the briefcase didn't slip from beneath his arm.

"If he kills anyone else, I'm going to hold you personally responsible."

Beckett released the man and then quickly left the office without another word. As he walked, he moved the folder he'd stolen from Peter Trout and pressed it to his chest, a smile forming on his face.

Chapter 45

REVEREND ALISTER CAMERON'S MILKED-OVER eyes stared up at Yasiv. The man's face was purple and bloated, and there was something wrong with his nose—it was pinched as if he'd just recently undergone plastic surgery. Lying on her side next to him was his wife, her hair covering her face.

Yasiv had seen a lot of death in his time, but it was the smell that got to him. The unmistakable sickly-sweet odor of death.

He swallowed hard, making sure that he didn't vomit all over the tarp and contaminate the crime scene. Breathing through his mouth, he turned to Detective Bradley, who had finally come forward.

"Two—"

"I think I'm going to be sick," Donald suddenly exclaimed. Yasiv's eyes went from the detective to Donald. The shirtless officer was doubled over, his trembling hand barely gripping the handle of the shovel.

"Oh, no you don't," Yasiv said, guiding the man away from the hole. "If you have to puke, do it over here. Not on the bodies, not on the evidence."

Confident that the bodies were out of spraying distance, Yasiv went back to the hole and inspected the Reverend's corpse more closely. As far as he could tell following a superficial examination, the blood hadn't come from him.

Which meant…

Yasiv brushed Holly Cameron's hair away from her face, revealing an incision in the side of her neck just below her jaw. It was covered in dried blood.

"It was her blood in the house," he said absently, not caring if Detective Bradley heard him or not. Moving back to Reverend Cameron's body, he noticed a thick substance protruding from each nostril. Yasiv ran the pad of his gloved finger beneath each.

The substance was hard to the touch.

"I think it's... I think it's glue," he said absently. To add further credence to this theory, he took a closer look at the man's eyes. They were bloodshot, and there were burst blood vessels on the skin surrounding the lids.

"Yeah, I think it is *glue*."

Yasiv pulled back and tried to take the scene in as a whole. The Reverend and his wife were completely naked, and the former seemed to be clutching his wife in some sort of macabre embrace. There was a rosary tucked under one shoulder, and Yasiv pulled it out and held it up for all to see.

"I guess God didn't save him," he muttered, before putting the rosary in a clear evidence bag. He sealed it and handed to the officer who had brought him the kit. The man took it, applied red tape to the seal and scribbled his initials on it to maintain the chain of custody.

That's when Yasiv noticed a second rosary, this one closer to Holly Cameron. He pulled it out and put it in another bag.

There might be prints on the crosses or some of the beads, he thought. But this wasn't the slam dunk he was looking for.

Yasiv leaned back once more, trying to identify anything that might lead back to Beckett.

"Nothing..."

But then he saw something, not on the bodies, but stuck to the corner of the tarp. It appeared to be a plastic tube or vial. Curious, Yasiv grabbed it, but it wouldn't budge.

"We should just leave the scene for CSU now," Detective Bradley informed him.

"Just a sec, I've got something here," Yasiv replied. Sweat dripped off his forehead and landed on Alister's swollen belly.

"Just leave it; CSU will collect any remaining evidence."

But Yasiv wasn't giving up, not now. As he readjusted his grip on the plastic vial, he realized it had lines on one side.

What the hell is this?

Grunting now, he tried to twist it free, but his gloves were too big and floppy to gain any real purchase.

"Sergeant Yasiv, get out of the hole," Detective Bradley said in a loud voice.

"Yeah, just a sec," Yasiv repeated out of the corner of his mouth.

Just as a hand came down on the shoulder, a big meaty paw, he twisted, and the object finally came free.

Holding it up to the light, Yasiv saw that it wasn't a vial at all, but a syringe. It was missing the plunger apparatus, and he hadn't initially noticed the metal needle, because it had pierced through the tarp and was embedded in the dirt.

"Yasiv—"

"I'm out, I'm out," he said, stepping away from the grave. He placed the syringe into a bag but didn't immediately hand this one-off. Instead, he stared at it intently.

"I've got you now, you son of a bitch," he whispered.

Detective Bradley immediately yanked the bag from his hand and gave it to the awaiting officer.

"What the fuck?"

"Sergeant Yasiv, can I talk to you over here for a moment?" the detective asked.

Yasiv didn't want to speak to the man; all he wanted to do was to take the syringe back to New York and get it processed for prints. But the officer had already disappeared with the three bags of evidence.

Oh sure, now *they move quickly.*

"Where's he going?" Yasiv asked, hooking a thumb toward the front of the house.

Detective Bradley didn't answer, instead, he indicated the side of the house again with one of his many chins.

"Sergeant Yasiv, over here."

Yasiv grimaced, but he reluctantly followed the man to the shaded area. In his mind, he was already picturing taking the evidence to the DA. Mark Trumbo might be reluctant to pursue the case against Beckett, but with the man's fingerprints on the potential murder weapon? He'd have no choice but to give Yasiv the resources he needed to put together a bulletproof case.

"We need to process the evidence right away," Yasiv said.

But the expression on the fat man's face indicated that this was the end of the line for him.

"I want to thank you for your help here, Sergeant Yasiv. You've been instrumental in finding the bodies. But now I think it's time for you to head back to New York. We'll take it from here."

Yasiv made a face.

"I think I'll wait for CSU to get here—there could be more evidence in the hole. And I think—"

"If there's any more evidence in there, CSU will find it. Right now, we need to keep the crime scene pristine."

Yasiv felt as if he was being accused of something and immediately got defensive.

"I was just trying to help—everyone was just standing around and—"

"Sergeant Yasiv, I know, and I appreciate your help."

Yasiv looked around. All eyes were on him now, and he knew that if he pushed any harder, he wasn't going to be asked to leave the premises, he'd be escorted.

Shit.

But if he just tucked his tail between his legs and left? Judging by the speed that these men worked, it could be months before he heard anything.

And Yasiv didn't have months.

He reluctantly removed his gloves and shook Detective Bradley's hand.

"Glad I could be of assistance," he said, holding the man's gaze a little longer than was comfortable.

With that, Yasiv grabbed his shirt and threw it on. It scratched his burnt skin something fierce, but he barely noticed as he made his way toward the front of the house.

"This is fucking bullshit," he whispered. "Absolute bullshit."

"What's that now?"

Yasiv looked up at the police officer who had spoken. The man was in the process of filling out some paperwork related to the three items in evidence bags that lay on the hood of his cruiser.

"Nothing," Yasiv replied, his eyes locked on those bags. *If I could just—*

"Sergeant Yasiv, wait up. I'll give you a lift," Officer Oliphant exclaimed as he appeared from behind the house.

Yasiv frowned.

Do I have a choice?

A bark drew his attention to the cadaver dogs that had been leashed to the side of the K-9 van. Without thinking, Yasiv walked over to them and reached down to scratch the closest dog's neck.

"Good boys," he said absently. "If only the rest of the department moved as quickly as you guys."

The dog leaned into him, and the leash banged against Yasiv's knuckles. And that's when a thought occurred to him. He looked up, but the man with the Oakley's, the handler, appeared to have taken a bathroom break; he was nowhere to be found.

They might take months to dust the syringe for prints. I can have it printed and in the system in New York in an hour, maybe even less.

Yasiv's thumb slipped over the leash, unclipping it from the dog's collar.

There's no going back now, he thought as he reached out and smacked the dog on the ass. *There's no going back.*

The dog yelped and then started to run toward the back of the house.

"Hey!" Officer Oliphant shouted. "Hey, grab him!"

Yasiv made a half-hearted attempt to wrangle the dog, but it was far too quick. The officer with the paperwork made a more valiant effort, but the dog eluded him, as well.

"Come on, get him!" Oliphant shouted as he turned to run. The other officer followed.

The second they were out of sight, Yasiv hurried to the hood of the now-abandoned squad car and stared at the three evidence bags. The two rosaries would be no help, he knew.

But the bag with the syringe?

If it had a fingerprint on it, it was enough to bring Beckett down for good.

There's no going back now, Yasiv. There's no going back...

Chapter 46

BECKETT RESISTED THE URGE to open the folder right then and there. Instead, he focused on getting the hell away from Peter Trout before the man realized that he'd been duped, that his precious 'sealed' case file had been stolen.

He hurried out of the building and then across campus. Beckett had just made it to the pathology department when he stopped cold.

Dr. Hollenbeck was speaking to the annoying temporary secretary again, blocking his path.

"Shit," he whispered under his breath.

"Speaking of Dr. Campbell, he's right behind you," the temp said with a sinister grin. Dr. Hollenbeck turned around, a slow and deliberate movement that gave Beckett just enough time to duck behind the corner.

Gripping the folder in both hands, he debated taking *The Sandlot* approach and just running home. But one could only put off their meeting with the Grim Reaper for so long.

With a labored sigh, Beckett forced a placating smile onto his face and stepped back into view.

"Dr. Hollenbeck, nice to see you again." Beckett shot lasers at the temp as he spoke and tried to slither past without confrontation.

But Dr. Hollenbeck stepped in his path.

"Yes, Dr. Campbell, I've been meaning to speak to you for some time now. There's been another complaint from one of your residents. First Maria not that long ago, and now Trevor."

Trevor? Who the hell is Trevor?

"I've dealt with it, Dr. Hollenbeck. It was all just a simple misunderstanding."

"Very good, but I would still like to have a conversation on the record about it. Just for safekeeping and it is procedure."

Beckett sighed.

"I would love to, but," he raised the folder and shook it dramatically, "perhaps it can wait for another time? I need to mark these tests."

"You should have your TA do that. It would be a good experience for her."

Beckett's smile wavered.

"Yeah, well, my TA is—"

"—in your office, actually," the temp finished for him.

Beckett snarled.

"Perfect, problem solved. Now, please, come into my office," Dr. Hollenbeck instructed, gesturing with an arthritic hand.

Beckett looked at the director's door, then at his own office.

Caught between Hitler and Mussolini... which to choose... which to choose...

"Fine, but it's gotta be quick," he said, reluctantly following in behind Dr. Hollenbeck.

Before entering, however, he turned back and mouthed the words 'fuck you' to the temp.

The temp replied by raising a manicured middle finger.

Why didn't I just slip her a twenty like I'd promised? Would it hurt to have one person—just one—on your side, Beckett?

***

"As I was saying," Dr. Hollenbeck began as he plopped himself down in an oversized chair. "This is your second complaint in the last month or so."

Where do these guys get their awesome chairs? Beckett wondered. *That dickhead Peter Trout has one made out of alpaca foreskin while Dr. Hollenbeck's looks like it's made from Koala pubes.*

"I would hate to write up any doctor, especially one of your esteem, Dr. Campbell. But, I'm afraid that if there are any more complaints, I will have no choice but to do just that."

He really is losing it. My esteem?

Beckett cleared his throat.

"As you know, I've been very stressed lately, what with Delores's father's passing and all."

Dr. Hollenbeck raised an eyebrow.

"Delores?"

"Yeah, the secretary. Her father died yesterday following routine surgery."

Even though the director nodded, it was clear that he had no idea who Delores was.

You know, the secretary that's been at that desk since I started here? The one that you've interacted with every day for the last ten years, maybe more?

"Yes, that was a shame, wasn't it?"

He has no fucking clue.

"Yeah, so as you can see, because of this workplace stress, I may have pushed my students too hard. But you know what they say, the harder you work, the better the results."

Beckett didn't know of anyone who said that, but it seemed fitting for someone like Dr. Hollenbeck.

"When I was a resident, I once worked a hundred-hour shift without stopping to even use the bathroom," Dr. Hollenbeck began, his words coming out painfully slowly. "You see, back then, we didn't have these fancy institutions, with all their..."

Roughly five minutes later, Beckett's own snoring woke him up.

Dr. Hollenbeck was so lost in his dementia-induced reverie that he didn't even appear to notice.

"So, yes I do understand pressure and stress. I would just ask that you take it easy on your residents moving forward in order to ensure that there are no more complaints."

"Yes, of course. Can I go now?"

The man nodded, and Beckett immediately moved toward the door.

"And Dr. Campbell?"

Beckett cringed and slid out of the man's office before he was reeled back in again. Ignoring the temp completely this time, he decided to head to his office and get the next lashing out of the way.

On the way, he opened the file and quickly skipped to the good part.

"You have to be shitting me," Beckett grumbled as he stepped into his office.

He found Suzan sitting on his chair, her feet on his desk.

"Suze, so nice of you to stop by. I'm sorry for keeping you waiting."

Suzan squinted at him.

"What the hell happened to your eye?"

Beckett recalled the envelope striking him like a ninja star and gently probed his eyelid. It was still swollen to the touch.

"Unfortunate occurrence involving a Thai hooker and a ping-pong ball. Now, would you kindly remove your feet from the Brazilian hardwood?"

To his surprise, Suzan did as he asked. But when she placed her left foot on the ground, Beckett noticed a subtle wince cross his girlfriend's scowling face.

"What happened to your ankle?" he asked, turning the tables on her.

"Got thrown off the Sybian."

Beckett chuckled and then grew serious.

"Suze, I'm sorry about last night. It's just that these assholes have been following me around ever since we got back from South Carolina. And with Delores's dad dying..."

Suzan shook her head.

"You might be able to lie to Dr. Hollenbeck, to your students, to your mother, but you can't lie to me, Beckett. What's really going on? You can talk to me—you can tell me anything."

Yeah, I severely doubt that.

And yet, the other part of what she'd said was undeniably true; he *couldn't* lie to her. Well, he *could*, but she'd know it.

With a sigh, Beckett plopped himself down in the chair across from her. Then he held up the folder he'd brought in with him.

"Dr. Gourde," he said at last.

"Dr. Gourde?"

Beckett opened the folder and held it out for her to see.

"As I told you at *Dorsia's*, Dr. Gourde is a piece of work. Killed three people so far, but just keeps getting shuffled around. And he's gay."

Suzan rolled her eyes.

"I don't care that he's gay."

"Me neither, but still. And get this, the tribunal found that Dr. Gourde was negligent *and* culpable in Mr. Leacock's death." Beckett looked at the file and drew Suzan's attention to a specific line. "Recommended action? *Nothing*. They say that even though Mr. Leacock died at NYU Med, he was operated on at a private clinic, so it's up to them to decide what to do. Can you imagine? Dr. Gourde's own private practice... that's like *Judge Dredd* being the judge, jury, and executioner in his own case."

Suzan made a face.

"That's messed up. Like, *really* messed up. But it's not your job to get involved. You promised Delores you'd find out what happened to her dad, and you did that. Now..." Suzan looked at him closely for a moment. "Ah, shit; let me guess, you can't let this go, can you?"

Beckett shook his head.

"You know, I should be pissed at you—I *am* pissed at you—but I also admire you, Beckett. You know what's right, what's good. Everyone else would just wash their hands of this, and they are. But you can't, can you? You just can't let bad people go."

You don't know the half of it.

"No, I can't," Beckett confirmed.

"That's admirable, Beckett. And it's rare."

Beckett shrugged.

Who is this person sitting across from me in my own, extremely uncomfortable chair?

Ever since getting back from South Carolina, Suzan's emotions had been all over the place.

"What can I say, I'm a modern-day Don Quixote."

Suzan's brow knitted.

"Don Quixote went insane and tried to spread chivalry across the land."

"Shit, really? Never read the thing."

"Not surprised. But I'll accept your apology, nonetheless. That being said, you still owe me a dinner."

"I took you to *Dorsia's* and it cost me—"

Suzan pulled a Beckett by clapping her hands and jumping to her feet.

"Anyways, we'll talk about this later. Right now, I have class." She hobbled over to him and kissed him on the cheek. "I'll see you tonight."

Beckett watched her go, more confused now than ever. There was something else about Dr. Gourde that he'd forgotten to mention, something important that skipped his mind.

"Wait, wait a second—you've got a class now? What time is it?"

Suzan rolled her wrist over and looked at her watch.

"4:05, why?"

Beckett's eyes suddenly bulged.

"Oh, shit! Oh, *shit!* I'm going to be late! Grant, I'm coming!"

Chapter 47

IT'S OKAY, IT'S OKAY, Yasiv told himself as he stared down at the plastic bag with the syringe inside. *The chain of command is still intact... it doesn't matter if the item is processed in New York City or South Carolina, so long as that seal is not broken.*

And yet, despite this knowledge, Yasiv couldn't help but feel that he'd made a horrible mistake by stealing the evidence and bringing it back to New York. But if it meant putting Dr. Beckett Campbell behind bars for murder, then so be it.

Yasiv was momentarily jarred out of his head by his phone ringing. It was the sixth or seventh time it had rung since landing in New York, and he didn't need to look at the number to know who was calling: Detective Boone Bradley.

You could answer it, say that you made a mistake, that you scooped the evidence up by accident. Then you could offer to go back to South Carolina and deliver it yourself.

There was no way that the detective would believe him, of course, but maybe that wouldn't matter. Maybe Detective Bradley would overlook the transgression based on the fact that Yasiv had basically busted the man's case wide open.

And then what? Then you're back at square one, waiting six months for prints. Who knows how many people Dr. Campbell will kill during that time? Who knows if you'll still have a job by then?

No, he conceded as he stared up at NYU Med and tapped the evidence bag on his palm. *It has to be now, and it has to be me.*

Yasiv lit one last cigarette and smoked it so quickly that he got a head rush. Then he gathered all his courage and stepped out of the car, evidence bag in hand.

There's no going back now, Yasiv. You better hope and pray that Beckett's fingerprints are all over this damn syringe or shit will really hit the fan.

Chapter 48

WHEN BECKETT FIRST PURCHASED his Tesla a couple of years ago, he never thought he'd have a use for *Insane Mode*. He was wrong.

Beckett implemented it now to cross the city, and in the process, he nearly killed more people than he had space for on his torso.

In the end, however, he made it to Dr. Gourde's private practice without running anyone over and in record time. There were no parking spaces available, but he didn't care. Beckett simply stopped in front of the entrance and hopped out.

He didn't have a plan, either, but knowing that it would only be minutes before Grant ended up on a gurney for Dr. Nordmeyer and her Sawzall like Mr. Leacock, Beckett went for broke.

Thankfully, the clinic was easy to locate and only required him to climb two flights of stairs. He burst through the frosted glass doors, and, huffing from exhaustion, rushed up to a lady seated behind the front desk.

A lady who looked suspiciously like the temp secretary back in the pathology department.

"I... need... Doctor... Gourde..."

The secretary leaned away from him, while her right hand slowly snaked toward the telephone.

"You want to make an appointment?"

Beckett placed both hands on the desk and shook his head.

"I need... Dr. Gourde..."

"Yeah, I got that. I can make an appointment for you, you just need to let me know —"

"No! *No!* I need him now!" Beckett nearly shouted after finally catching his breath.

"I'm sorry, but Dr. Gourde is in surgery at the moment and cannot be disturbed. If you'd like to make an appointment, please take a seat with the others."

Beckett turned around and, to his horror, realized that the waiting room was full of people. Most seemed to be in their mid-seventies or early eighties, with a plethora of walkers and canes leaning up against the peach-colored walls.

Beckett was reminded of Mr. Leacock who'd come in for a disk replacement and had come out dead. He waved his arms over his head.

"Get out of here!"

A handful of blue-haired women exchanged looks, but nobody moved.

"No, no, look, you have to get out of here. This isn't... this isn't..."

...working. These poor people... they have no idea what Dr. Gourde has in store for them.

"What seems to be the problem, son?" an old man with thick spectacles and a lopsided mustache demanded.

Beckett licked his lips and decided to change tactics.

"No problem, no problem, it's just... it's just the Walmart on 51st Street is giving away free Depends and drastically reduced prune juice. They're practically giving the stuff away!"

Confident that he'd done his best to save what remained of these old peoples' lives, Beckett turned back to the secretary. For some reason, she was holding a phone out to him.

"Dr. Gourde—" he began before searing hot pain suddenly engulfed his entire left eye.

It wasn't a phone in the secretary's hand, Beckett realized as he doubled over in agony, but pepper spray.

"I'll spray you again," the woman warned. Beckett instinctively brought a hand up to shield his face. "If you move, I'll spray you again. Don't even think about moving—security is on their way."

Beckett held up both hands as if to say, *I'm not doing anything*. But that was a lie.

He slunk away from the desk and then started to run, half-blind, down the hallway towards where he expected the operating rooms to be located.

Both eyes watering now, he had to use his fingers to grope the wall and feel his way along. Thankfully, the secretary didn't stay true to her promise; for some reason, she didn't spray him again, for which Beckett was exceedingly grateful.

The first set of doors he burst through led to an empty operating room, and Beckett cursed. Eyes still leaking profusely, he staggered through the next set of doors.

These proved more fruitful. Even though he was seeing triple, he was fairly certain that there was at least one doctor in the room and two nurses. And they were all looking at him.

"Don't do this!" he cried.

The doctor stepped forward, and Beckett instantly knew that this man was Dr. Gourde.

"You can't be in here! *Security!*"

Beckett waved him away, still blinking like a maniac.

"Please, don't do this," Beckett repeated.

He glanced over the doctor's shoulder and saw Grant lying on the operating table, a mask over his nose and mouth.

Dr. Gourde stepped forward.

"You need to leave, now. We are about to operate."

Beckett finally managed to stand up straight and stared at the doctor with his one good eye.

"Please," he pleaded. "That's my lover and I didn't get to kiss him goodbye this morning. It's bad luck if I don't kiss him goodbye. Take the mask off... I *need* to kiss him."

Chapter 49

DUNBAR WASN'T TOO PROUD to apologize. In fact, unlike others in his profession, he believed that apologizing was a sign of strength and not weakness.

And yet, he knew that he was going to have to swallow more than his pride to get his job back.

Something had happened to Sergeant Yasiv while searching for Wayne Cravat. The man had gone off his rocker and had decided to put Dr. Beckett Campbell squarely in his sights.

Winston Trent had been a horrible human being, as had Bob Bumacher and Craig Sloan. Even if Dr. Beckett Campbell was responsible for their deaths, which Dunbar found extremely doubtful at this point, what did it matter? The world was a better place without them, and while *Vigilante Justice* wasn't high on Dunbar's annual charitable donation list, he knew that when bad things happened to bad people, sometimes it was best to just look the other way.

He also knew that, more often than not, they just went unpunished. Case in point, what had happened to him when he was younger—the man responsible was still out there somewhere. Dunbar would shed zero tears if that piece of work ended up on the wrong end of a .22.

But Dunbar wasn't ready to give up on Yasiv or the NYPD—not just yet. If he wanted to join the SVU one day, he had to patch things up with the sergeant. He had to make it right.

As luck would have it, Dunbar actually passed Yasiv on the way to 62nd precinct. To his surprise, however, the sergeant drove right by the police station without even slowing. Confused, Dunbar decided to follow him. Fifteen minutes later, he found himself in the NYU Med parking lot.

What the hell is he doing here? Dunbar wondered as he watched smoke filter out of Yasiv's open window. *Is he here to confront Beckett? To arrest him?*

It took an incredible amount of willpower to just sit there and wait, but eventually, his patience paid off. A disheveled Sergeant Henry Yasiv finally emerged from his car, clutching something close to his chest.

Confused, Dunbar cautiously stepped out into the midday sun. He considered approaching his ex-boss, but the look on the man's face—his bloodshot eyes, his sallow cheeks—convinced him otherwise. Instead, he kept his distance, hoping, for his friend's sake, that he wasn't going to do anything stupid.

But the longer he watched Sergeant Yasiv, the more he was convinced that the man had *already* done something that was incredibly dumb. Something that they would both live to regret.

Chapter 50

DR. GOURDE'S FACE SUDDENLY changed. Beckett wasn't sure if it was the realization that Grant was gay, or simply the complete absurdity of the situation, but whatever the reason, the doctor stepped aside. Thinking that this might just be a fleeting moment of compassion, Beckett quickly pushed by him and approached Grant.

With everyone looking onward, Beckett pulled the mask off his resident's nose and mouth.

"Grant, wake up," he muttered. Grant's eyes fluttered, but he didn't stir. "Wake up."

Beckett raised his head and gave the onlookers a weak smile. "For fuck sake," he whispered. "Don't make me do this."

But it appeared as if he had no choice.

With an exasperated sigh, Beckett puckered his lips and leaned in close for a kiss. His mouth had just barely grazed Grant's when the man's eyes snapped open and Beckett pulled back.

"Beckett? What the fuck are you doing?" Grant demanded.

In one smooth motion, Beckett wiped his lips with the back of his arm, and then slapped Grant across the face. Someone in the room gasped.

"You left without kissing me this morning. How *dare* you."

Still suffering from the lingering sedation, Grant remained incredibly confused, and he simply stared at Beckett.

"You never should have left," Beckett barked, once again slapping him across the cheek.

"Okay, that's enough," a security guard who had entered the room sometime during Beckett's unrequited romance ordered. He grabbed Beckett's arm and pulled. At first, Beckett resisted, but then he thought better of it and used their combined momentum to yank Grant into a seated position.

"No, he can't get up, he's got surgery," Dr. Gourde said, desperate to regain control of the situation.

Grant blinked and then somehow managed to rise to his feet on his own. Still dazed, the man looked around, spending at least five seconds observing the faces of every person in the operating room.

Eventually, he focused on only one: Beckett's.

"How dare you," Grant hissed. "How dare you slap me in front of all these people."

Before Beckett realized what was happening, Grant reared back and struck him across the face. The blow was so powerful that he stumbled backward. It also re-ignited the pain from the pepper spray and envelope ninja star.

"Jesus," Beckett whispered, holding the left side of his face in his hands.

"How dare you," Grant said, lunging at him again. Thankfully, one of the nurses intervened before his hand reached Beckett's inflamed cheek.

"That's enough," an enraged Dr. Gourde said. "You two, get the fuck out of my operating room."

Beckett smiled and apologized, hooking his arm through Grant's as they started toward the door together.

"And I'm still billing you for the operative time!"

"That was close," Beckett said once they were out of the operating room. He cast a glance towards the waiting area, and a small smile crept onto his face when he saw it was now empty.

"You're telling me," Grant muttered, still clearly feeling the effects of the anesthetics. "You're telling me."

***

After two cups of strong coffee, Grant was no worse for wear. And yet, judging by the way he was slumped in the passenger seat of Beckett's Tesla, it was clear that he was still sour.

"Hey, I'm sorry I was late," Beckett offered.

Grant grunted.

Not knowing what to do, Beckett tossed the folder he'd stolen from Peter Trout on the man's lap. Grant opened it and started to read. Two minutes later, he raised his eyes.

"This is supposed to make me feel better? You... you *kissed* me."

Beckett shrugged.

"Why are you complaining? Aren't you on Grindr?"

Grant shook his head.

"No, I'm not on Grindr."

"Isn't that how you found out about Dr. Pumpkinhead?"

"Well, yeah, but I was just looking into the man like you asked."

Beckett puckered his lips and made a smooching sound.

"Well, it wasn't a bad kiss. It wasn't the best, either, but, hey." He shrugged. "Anyways, I'm not really sure why you're so pissed. I got to you in time, didn't I?"

"Barely."

"Barely is just a synonym for punctual. Did you read what's in the folder? Did you see what Dr. Gourde did to Delores's father?"

Grant nodded, and his eyes drifted down to Dr. Karen Nordmeyer's notes in his lap.

"Darien Leacock recently underwent C2 to C3 spinal fusion for a degenerated disk. The fusion was incomplete, and none of the hardware was anchored into bone. Instead, screws were applied to the soft tissue of the neck and throat." Grant skipped ahead. "Cause of death was exsanguination due to a severed carotid artery. As a result of the presence of extensive inflammation, it is likely that the injury was sustained during surgery, and Mr. Leacock survived for as long as he did only because a surgical sponge that was left in his neck."

"Talk about surgical precision."

Grant ignored the comment and flipped through several more pages.

"The tribunal... they're not even going to report this? He's... he's just going to keep running his private practice? That's crazy."

Beckett nodded.

"Yep. So, technically, I saved your life. Just saying."

Grant scowled.

"At best, Dr. Gourde is a horrible surgeon."

Beckett cleared his throat and nodded.

"At best. And at worst?" He paused. His fingers were tingling so badly now that he had to focus on gripping the steering wheel to make sure that his hands didn't slip off. "At worst, Grant, he's a murderer."

PART V

Irrefutable Evidence

Chapter 51

YASIV HURRIED DOWN THE hall to the laboratory that they'd used during the Skeleton King case when the precinct lab was overloaded. He moved quickly, trying to minimize the chances of seeing Dr. Campbell. He knew the odds of an encounter in a place this large were exceedingly rare, but he couldn't risk it. Not with the evidence bag clutched to his chest.

Eventually, he found the door he was looking for. Just as he was about to knock, the phone in Yasiv's pocket buzzed.

It was Detective Bradley again, and he let it go to voice mail.

No going back...

Yasiv took a deep breath and knocked on the door. When there was no answer, he knocked again. And again. On the fifth such knock, the door was finally opened by a man with long dark hair tucked behind his ears. He peered out suspiciously at Yasiv behind thick spectacles.

"Hi," Yasiv said, pulling out his badge and showing it to the man.

"What can I do for you, officer?" the lab tech asked.

"For starters, you can let me in."

The man nodded and Yasiv quickly slipped inside and closed the door behind him.

"My name's Sergeant Yasiv of the 62nd precinct. I'm here with a very... *sensitive*... request."

Lab guy's eyes narrowed.

"Yes, of course, what can I help you with?"

Yasiv raised the evidence bag to eye level.

"I need you to run fingerprint tests on this, and I need to keep the chain of command intact. Can you do that?"

The man nodded.

"Of course; we have a special room for evidence just down the hall. It used to be temporary, but after the Church of Liberation massacre, it became permanent. Just follow me."

The lab tech held the door open and indicated for Yasiv to exit the lab. After a furtive glance up and down the hallway, Yasiv stepped out and the tech followed.

They walked for less than a minute before hanging a right and ending up in front of a secure-looking door. The lab tech scanned his ID card, then had to punch a code into the lock. It beeped and unlocked.

This level of security eased Yasiv's nerves a little. Even though Beckett wasn't the most popular man on campus, he'd been working there for some time and knew his way around. And there were always favors... the world seemed to work on favors. If the doctor managed to find out about all this, it was highly unlikely that he'd be able to gain access to the evidence.

Yasiv entered a small room about the size of his office back at the precinct. Off to the right was a fume hood of some sort, while two computer monitors, and a microscope rested near the opposite wall.

"You're just gonna have to complete one of these requisition sheets there before we do anything," the tech instructed.

"Of course," Yasiv said quickly, grabbing the paper from his hand. He filled out his personal information, including badge number, and then checked off that he wanted fingerprint analysis performed. He briefly debated asking for DNA retrieval as well but figured that this would take too long.

If he needed it later, for a trial, perhaps, he could always ask for it then.

When it came to where the evidence was obtained, Yasiv hesitated. In the end, he decided to keep it ambiguous and wrote: gravesite.

Satisfied, he handed the requisition sheet back and the tech gave it a once over.

"All right, looks good. We can leave the specimen here for now. This room will be locked, and the chain of custody will be maintained."

Yasiv nodded and placed the bag in the fume hood.

"Okay, what next?" he asked, annoyed that this was taking as long as it was.

"In order to move forward, I need to get my supervisor's signature."

"I'll wait."

The tech shook his head.

"Unfortunately, he's already left for the day."

Yasiv groaned and scratched his forehead. When he pulled his hand away, there were flakes of skin beneath his fingernails, a reminder of his time digging in the sun.

"Can you call him? Get him to come in? As I said, this is sensitive, but maybe I didn't stress how important was to get it done as soon as possible."

The man shook his head and once again gestured toward the door.

"I understand your concerns, but I simply cannot open that bag until my supervisor signs the form. And that will not happen until tomorrow."

Yasiv grimaced. He thought about arguing, but judging by the man's face, he knew that wasn't going to get him anywhere. The irony of taking the syringe from South Carolina and bringing it to New York primarily because he was concerned about the turnaround time down south, and now getting sandbagged, was not beyond him.

"Fine," he spat. "What time is your supervisor going to come in in the morning, then?"

"Seven thirty."

Yasiv reached for the door and opened it. But before he stormed out, the sergeant turned back and leveled his eyes at the tech's.

"Good. I'll be here at seven fifteen to meet you guys. And don't forget what I said about this being sensitive and a priority. If anything goes wrong, I'm going to hold you personally responsible."

Chapter 52

AFTER DROPPING GRANT OFF, Beckett headed home. He tried to force everything that had happened recently out of his mind by focusing on preparing a nice dinner for him and Suzan. First, he vacuum-sealed two fresh USDA Prime rib eyes and dropped them in the sous vide bath at 129°. Then he took out a bag of Brussel sprouts and began chopping them in half. His phone rang and, still chopping and only half paying attention, he put it on speaker.

"Brussel sprouts are just like tiny little alien heads, don't you think?" When there was no immediate reply, he stopped chopping. "Suzan?"

"No, sorry, it's not Suzan, it's Delores. I don't mean to bother you at home, Dr. Campbell, but I just can't... I haven't slept since my dad died. I tried calling the morgue to find out about the autopsy, but they won't tell me anything. They keep saying that the report is sealed, that I have to put in a formal request with the ombudsman or something. I don't even know what that is, Dr. Campbell."

The poor woman broke into sobs and Beckett set his knife down on the counter.

"Delores, I said I would look into what happened with your father, and I meant it."

"But—but how could this happen? It was a simple surgery. I looked into the surgeon, into Dr. Gourde, and I found out that this isn't the first time that he's done something like this. How is it possible that he keeps operating on people when he makes these kinds of mistakes?"

Beckett closed his eyes and pinched the bridge of his nose. He felt another headache coming on.

"I don't know, but you're right; he shouldn't be operating. I can't promise you an insurance payout or anything like that, but what I can promise you, is that Dr. Gourde is never going to operate again."

"I don't care about the money," Delores replied. "All I care about is making sure that this doctor doesn't kill anyone else."

Beckett ground his teeth.

"Delores, I promise you that Dr. Gourde won't kill again."

"Thank you, Dr. Campbell. Thank you."

After saying goodbye, Beckett stared at the knife that he'd been using to chop the Brussel sprouts.

"Fuck it," he said, reaching for his phone again. Instead of dialing, though, he fired off a quick text.

Suzan, something's come up. I'm sorry, but I'm out for dinner. Steaks are in the bath. Please, help yourself. Don't hate me. Beckett.

Knowing that she would reply instantly, Beckett shut off his phone.

Delores was right; Dr. Gourde shouldn't be allowed to operate again, and there was only one way that Beckett knew how to stop the man permanently.

He hurried upstairs and changed into black track pants and a dark hoodie. When he stopped to inspect himself in the mirror, he cringed.

His left eye was swollen and there were scratches on his cheek from where Grant had slapped him. With the hood pulled up over his head as it was, Beckett looked more like Sloth from The Goonies than a quasi-respected doctor.

Yeah, well, this ain't no fashion show, my man.

Beckett went to the top drawer of his dresser next and retrieved his black case. Inside, he confirmed that he had two syringes preloaded with midazolam and a fresh scalpel. There was also a pair of black zip ties that he'd found a few days ago and thought might come in handy buried beneath the other tools.

Beckett knew that what he was thinking of doing was incredibly risky given the fact that Sergeant Yasiv was on his ass, but he had made a promise to Delores.

Yet, he'd be lying if he said that was the only reason; the urge to kill had gotten stronger even though it had only been a handful of days since he'd murdered Alister and Holly Cameron.

To say this worried him was an understatement.

Beckett knew that it was in his best interest to lay low for a few weeks, to have that 'normal' dinner with Suzan as he'd originally planned.

Except he was anything but normal, and any hope of a 'normal' life had disappeared the moment he'd had that fateful encounter with serial killer Craig Sloan.

The night the man's skull met a large stone, up close and personal, multiple times.

***

Beckett waited in the alleyway until the nurse finished her cigarette. When she flicked the butt away, he counted to ten and then hurried to the door. As he'd expected, this wasn't the nurse's last smoke of the night, and she'd left it unlocked.

Beckett slipped inside, but instead of heading directly to the second floor, he walked down a flight of stairs and huddled out of sight beneath the staircase.

The minutes and then hours ticked by. Just after nine in the evening, the nurse returned and smoked her final cigarette. This time when she closed the door, she made sure to lock it. With a sigh, the heavy-set woman grunted her way back upstairs and then roughly ten minutes later, the lights clicked off.

Still, Beckett waited. It was only when the hour reached ten, did he finally spring into action.

Moving silently, he climbed to the second floor. In addition to locking the staircase exit, the nurse had done the same to the door to Dr. Gourde's private practice. But this was the back door and security wasn't as tight as Beckett expected the front to be. All it took was wedging a doorjamb he found into the space between the door and the frame and delivering a swift kick, and it popped open. There didn't even appear to be any permanent damage to either the door or the locking mechanism.

Once inside, Beckett stood perfectly still and listened.

He heard nothing.

Well, if Dr. Gourde gets away with murder, I'm going to have to report him to the medical board for having the worst security ever in a place that contains enough anesthetic to knock out a city block.

It took him a moment to orient himself, but eventually, he identified the two operating rooms to the right of Mrs. Pepper Spray's desk, and a series of offices to the left. With his back pressed against the wall, Beckett hurried across the waiting area to the desk and then hunkered beneath it. On a whim, he opened the top drawer and then cringed when the handle rattled noisily. Beckett waited, and then, confident that he hadn't been heard, he reached inside.

A small smile crept onto his face as he retrieved the bottle of pepper spray. Thinking that it might come in handy later, Beckett slipped it into his pocket.

Even though the only sounds he'd heard were of his own doing, Beckett knew that Dr. Gourde was more than likely still here. Most serial murderers were narcissists, which meant that the doctor would insist on being the last one to leave *his* practice.

This was confirmed by the bluish glow of a computer monitor emanating from the largest office at the end of the narrow hallway.

Beckett was about to head toward the light when he heard someone grunt, followed by the sound of a pneumatic chair piston firing.

Fuck.

He ducked back behind the wall and waited. Footsteps started toward him, and he tensed his thumb on the plunger of the midazolam-filled syringe.

But he didn't have to use the drugs, not yet, anyway.

A door opened and then closed. Beckett counted to ten, then risked peeking out again.

Bathroom... the man just went to the shitter.

Knowing that he didn't have much time, Beckett scampered down the hall and slid into the office. As predicted, Dr. Gourde's desk was huge, as was the computer monitor resting atop it. Behind the desk was a wall of windows looking out into the alleyway that he'd entered the building from.

But none of this held Beckett's attention. No, his eyes were locked on the man's chair.

It was throne-like, with plush sides made of perforated leather that looked taken straight from a Rolls-Royce Phantom driver's seat.

"What is with you guys and these fucking chairs," he whispered. Then he scolded himself.

Focus, you ass clown. Focus.

Despite what he'd uncovered about Dr. Gourde, Beckett still needed more proof that the man wasn't just the world's worst doctor. He needed to *know* that Gourde was killing people on purpose.

To this end, Beckett scanned the bookshelf leaning against the wall. While having multiple copies of Ayn Rand's *Atlas Shrugged*, let alone the sequels, should be a criminal offense, this did not satisfy the high burden of proof Beckett required. With a grunt, he turned to the man's computer next. But to his dismay, the paranoid doctor had locked his computer even to go for a shit.

"Dammit."

As a last resort, Beckett pulled the top drawer of the desk open. There was nothing inside but two Mont Blanc pens and some stationary with Dr. Gourde's letterhead.

He tried the second drawer next, but it was locked. Intrigued, he dropped onto all fours and inspected the enclosure. It was rudimentary, at best. Beckett was fairly good at picking locks and took to the challenge readily, despite the pressing timeline.

Reaching back into the first drawer, he pulled out one of the pens and took the cap off. Then he shoved the narrow end into the lock. With a three count, Beckett took a deep breath and drove his palm against the butt end of the pen. There was a metallic pop, and he froze.

There was no sound from the bathroom down the hall.

Confident that Dr. Gourde hadn't heard him, Beckett opened the drawer. He didn't know what to expect—he *wanted* a confession letter—but costume jewelry? That was perhaps the last thing he thought he would find.

What the hell?

His first thought was that Dr. Gourde was moonlighting as some sort of pawn shark, but that didn't make sense. A man like him would never stoop to that level.

Beckett rummaged through the drawer, shoving cheap watches around, sifting through crap that looked like it had been purchased from the bargain bin at Le Chateau.

"Come on, come on. Gimme something."

Frustrated now, Beckett shoved a gold watch to the back of the drawer. It banged loudly, and he became perfectly still.

"Sam? Is that you?" Dr. Gourde hollered from the bathroom.

Beckett held his breath while the toilet flushed. He only had seconds to decide what to do before the doctor barged through the office door. As he contemplated his next course of action, Beckett's eyes focused on the watch that had given him away. It had flipped over, revealing an engraved silver plate on the inside of the band that read: *DML*.

And then, at that moment, it clicked.

DML... Darien M. Leacock.

This wasn't a drawer full of pawned jewelry, but a drawer full of souvenirs and trophies of the people Dr. Gourde had killed.

Beckett retrieved his syringe and then started to crawl out from beneath the desk.

Yes, he realized, *Dr. Gourde did know what he was doing. He was killing people and, more importantly, he was doing it on purpose.*

From down the hall, he heard water running, followed by a door opening and then more footsteps. Beckett used this time to move toward the bookshelf, which was out of sight from the half-open office door.

He took one breath, two, and just as Dr. Gourde stepped into the office and he was preparing to lunge, Beckett heard another sound.

Only this one wasn't coming from *inside* but *outside*—from the alley.

Beckett's eyes were instinctively drawn to the squeal of screeching tires. And that's when he saw the black Lincoln speed off. It could've been *any* Lincoln of course, but Beckett knew better; it was *the* Lincoln.

You gutless little—

"What the fuck?" Dr. Gourde roared. "What the fuck are you doing in here?"

Chapter 53

BECKETT INSTINCTIVELY JUMPED AT the man, leading with the syringe. But Dr. Gourde was primed and ready, and he stepped to one side, while at the same time, knocking Beckett off his feet with a two-handed swipe. The syringe flew against the bookcase and then rolled out of sight.

"You're trying to rob me? You're trying to rob *me*?" an incredulous Dr. Gourde demanded.

Beckett turned onto his stomach, trying to hide his face, all the while his mind was racing.

The Lincoln was here... they know, Beckett. You can't kill him. Not now. They know.

That was the only thing that made sense.

They knew about him, and about what he'd done—about the people he'd killed.

Beckett slipped his hand into the front pocket of his sweatshirt, but after struggling to pull the black case out, he knew that there was no time to retrieve another syringe.

Fuck!

He pushed himself onto all fours, and something dug into his thigh and he winced. It was something cylindrical and hard, and—

The pepper spray!

In a flash, he rolled onto his side and pulled the pepper spray free. That's when the maniacal doctor leaped, his hands and fingers outstretched and aimed at Beckett's throat.

"Shit!"

The caustic spray struck Dr. Gourde in the face and the man's entire body seemed to contract inward. With a shriek, he landed on Beckett's chest, knocking the wind out of him with his elbow.

Dr. Gourde clawed at his face, making it easy for Beckett to shove him off to one side, even though he was struggling to breathe.

Still trying to coax his diaphragm back to life, Beckett scampered on all fours, desperately searching for the syringe.

Where'd you go, where the hell did you—

He finally managed to suck in a massive breath, then immediately moaned in near ecstasy.

But none of this helped him find the syringe; the only thing remotely close that Beckett could see was the top of the Mont Blanc pen.

Where are you?

He cast a glance over at Dr. Gourde, who was wiping at his eyes and starting to recover and sit up.

"You tried to rob *me!*"

I tried to do more than that, Beckett thought. *But that's gonna have to wait.*

"I'll kill you, I'll fucking kill you. Do you know who I am?"

Dr. Gourde's words were becoming more cogent, and Beckett knew that he was running out of time.

He debated spraying the man again, maybe even kicking him in the ribs for good measure, but instead, Beckett simply bowed his head, tucked his chin to his chest, and ran.

***

The black Lincoln was gone now, but the good news was that the night air had yet to erupt in sirens. Beckett supposed that was one saving grace about hunting killers; they were as averse to getting the cops involved as he was. Still, he couldn't risk lingering outside Dr. Gourde's office for much longer.

Beckett slid behind the wheel of his Tesla and grunted when the pain in his ribs flared. He managed one deep breath, then slammed his hands down on the wheel.

"What the hell were you thinking, Beckett? There could be cameras in there. And the syringe... you lost the damn syringe!"

Thankfully, he was still wearing gloves and there would be no prints on it, but there were only so many places that one could get midazolam from—it's not as if it was a common street drug. If Dr. Gourde was half as smart as he thought he was, all the man had to do was put in a few inquiries, and...

"Stupid, stupid, stupid!" Beckett shouted as he slammed his hands on the wheel again.

With Yasiv out for blood and these fucking goons in the Lincoln after you, you still thought it was a good idea to kill Dr. Gourde?

But that was the thing; he *hadn't* been thinking.

Beckett teased the leather case out of his sweatshirt pocket and tossed it in the glove box. He was about to drive off when a thought occurred to him and he pulled it back out again. Instead of grabbing the final syringe or scalpel, however, he opted for the zip ties and shoved them into his jean pocket.

As he shifted the car into drive, in his mind, Beckett could still hear the Lincoln's tires squealing.

They knew I was here, and somehow, they knew what I was going to do.

Beckett might have no recourse when it came to Sergeant Yasiv, but the frat boys in the black car?

His eyes flicked to the clock in the dash and he saw that it was coming up on eleven fifteen.

Well, he just might be able to do something about *them*.

And this time, he knew exactly where they were going to be, and not the other way around.

Chapter 54

BECKETT LOCATED THE BLACK Lincoln with the garbage bag-covered window parked outside twenty-one fifty-five Hastings Rd. as he'd expected. It wasn't hard to notice, either; other than his Tesla, it was the only other vehicle in the expansive lot.

"What the hell is this place?" Beckett wondered as he looked up at the estate before him.

Twenty-one fifty-five Hastings Rd. was a massive, three-story stone building with a majestic staircase leading up to two wooden double doors.

Beckett had never seen such a place in New York; he didn't think they existed. It looked like a castle that belonged in Germany or the Czech Republic, not in New York.

Deciding to keep a low profile, he started slowly up the steps, his eyes fixed on the multitude of windows above the doors. All the lights were off inside, and there didn't appear to be any movement from within.

And this night just keeps getting stranger...

Beckett shielded his eyes with his hands and pressed his nose against the glass beside the door. And then he stepped backward as one of them started to open.

There goes the element of surprise. Way to go, Beckett.

Rather than bolting, Beckett stood his ground, taking up a defensive posture.

Here goes—

"You?" he exclaimed.

The young man holding the door open swallowed hard and lowered his eyes.

"Dr. Campbell, this is a black-tie event," he said quietly.

Beckett looked down at his black tracksuit.

"Really? That's what you're pissed about? That I'm not dressed appropriately?"

Without thinking, Beckett reached into his pocket and pulled out two black zip ties.

"Here's my black tie—two of them. Now be a good boy and put them on. We need to have a little chat."

The man looked at the zip ties, but when he didn't make any effort to reach for them, Beckett strode forward.

And then he hesitated.

The castle wasn't dark inside as he'd first thought, nor was it empty.

The interior was dimly lit, but the reason why Beckett couldn't see the light from outside was that there appeared to be some sort of paint on the inner pane of the windows.

And then there were the people. Dozens of them, maybe even fifty in total, all sporting fancy suits, or long, flowing dresses.

"What in the Christ?"

Beckett shook his head, wondering if the pepper spray that had burned his eye had leeched into his brain.

"What the fuck is this place?"

"This is DNR; please, Dr. Campbell, enter," the frat boy at the door instructed.

Beckett looked at him for a moment.

"It was a rhetorical question, dumb ass," he said, and yet, Beckett was compelled to enter.

His eyes naturally drifted upward to the massive chandelier in the foyer. It looked as if it cost as much as his entire house. Beckett took another step, moving deeper into the strange castle, and then his gaze was drawn downward by an approaching man.

He was wearing an immaculate black suit that had tails at the back, and a crisp white shirt complete with a bowtie.

"Beckett, I didn't know if you'd come," he said, a smirk on his face. "But I'm glad you did."

"Dr. Swansea? What in the holy fuck is going on here?"

Chapter 55

SERGEANT YASIV COULDN'T RISK going back to his office to sleep, even though he desperately needed it. He didn't even want to go back to his house in case the DA had it under surveillance. At this point, there was no doubt in Yasiv's mind that Detective Bradley had reached out to his superiors.

It was only a matter of time before they came for him, and when they did, Yasiv wanted to be ready.

He walked back to his car instead and climbed behind the wheel.

I'm just going to wait here all night until the tech guy's supervisor comes in. Then I'm going to get the prints and go back to see DA Mark Trumbo.

Yasiv had just lit a cigarette when a shadow crossed his windshield. His hand instinctively went to the gun on his hip, but the man who approached put his hands up.

"Hank? It's me, it's Dunbar."

Yasiv blinked several times and then let go of his gun. Yet, he only rolled his window down halfway.

"Yeah?" he asked hesitantly.

Dunbar's head dropped.

"I just wanted to apologize for earlier, Hank. I don't know what I was thinking. It's just that... well, with what happened with Winston Trent and Brent Hopper... I mean..."

Yasiv reluctantly rolled his window down all the way.

"It's all right, Dunbar. I get it."

Dunbar suddenly lifted his gaze, revealing red and watery eyes.

"I don't think you do, Hank. Look, I've been going to these meetings at the church to talk about things, trying to work things out."

"You mean the church that Winston, Wayne, and Brent went to?" The words came out as more of an accusation than an inquisition. "Why?"

Dunbar paused.

"Because I needed to talk to someone, Hank. And the guy who runs the show? Frank Burnett? He's a good man. He doesn't judge people, he just tries to help."

Yasiv nodded, even though he was struggling to follow. He knew of Dunbar's past, of what happened to him at camp all those years ago, but this hardly seemed like the place to hash out more details.

And he wasn't in the mood for a hugfest.

"Is it... is it helping?" Yasiv asked, mostly because he was unsure of what else to say.

Dunbar shrugged again.

"I dunno, maybe. Probably not based on what happened between us the other day. But the thing is... Frank got me thinking. The thing he does best is listen, so, with this in mind, I went to see Beckett—I went to his house to speak to him, but mostly just to listen. And I can tell you that he isn't who you think he is. Beckett's a good man, Hank, he's a doctor and—"

Yasiv's face suddenly went red.

"Wait, you went to see *him*? You went to see Dr. Campbell?"

"Yeah, I had to—"

"Why would you do that?" Yasiv demanded. "For Christ's sake, Dunbar, he's the prime suspect in half a dozen homicides... and you went to *see* him? For what? To tip him off?"

Dunbar suddenly became defensive.

"To tip him off? He already knew you were gunning for him, Hank—everybody in the city knows it by now. But the thing that gets me most, is that you got a search warrant for his house and never told me. You never even mentioned your suspicions the whole time we were working together on the Wayne Cravat case. How many times have you told me that I was the only one you could trust after what happened with all the other detectives that Ken Smith had in his pocket? Ten? A dozen? And yet you never said a single thing to me about this whole mess... this *vendetta* of yours."

Yasiv was seething now and he gripped the steering wheel tightly in both hands.

"And why do you think that is? No, don't answer that. *This is why I didn't tell you*, and this is why you'll never be in the SVU—because you let your emotions cloud your judgment. I didn't tell you, Dunbar, because I thought you'd blow the whole case. And guess what? You probably did."

Dunbar threw his hands up.

"There *is* no case, Hank—there never was. You made all this shit up in your head because you're desperate to find Wayne Cravat. You want someone to blame for him going missing, for the injustices done to the man. And I get that because I'm pretty sure he's completely innocent, too. But whatever happened to Wayne, Beckett had nothing to do with it. This is just a... a... a *witch hunt*. Nothing more, nothing less."

"Get the fuck away from my car, Dunbar."

"So, it's going to be like that, is it? Now you're going to blame me? Why? Because I actually tried to talk to Beckett? Something you're just too proud to do? Look, if you're so desperate for someone to blame, why not look in the mirror, Yasiv? After all, you were the one who brought Wayne Cravat in for the murder of Bentley Thomas. If you hadn't done that, if you hadn't soiled the man's name, plastered it all over the media, he'd probably still be hanging out at the trailer park with his buddies Winston and Brent. Oh? Didn't think I knew about that, did you? Yeah, well, I do. So, instead of a witch hunt for Beckett, why not look at what you did, at yourself, for once?"

"Get away from my car."

"You know what? Maybe I'm not the one who needs to talk to someone, but you do."

"Dunbar, get the fuck away from my car!" Yasiv shouted. "Get away from my car before I put you in handcuffs!"

Dunbar stepped away from the open window.

"I thought you were my friend, Hank, but you're just like the rest of them. You're just like all the corrupt cops that Ken Smith had on his payroll. No, you know what? You're *not* like that. You're worse. You're worse because I didn't trust them, I wasn't friends with them. But I trusted you and I was friends with you. But you lied to me and manipulated me, Hank."

With that, Dunbar spun around and started to walk away.

Yasiv debated getting out of the car and chasing after him, maybe coming through on his promise to arrest him, but he couldn't bring himself to do it.

Instead, the sergeant of 62nd precinct simply brought the heels of his hands to his eyes and started to rub them furiously.

What am I doing here? What the hell am I doing?

Chapter 56

"DR. SWANSEA? YOU GONNA tell me what's going on here? I feel like I'm an extra on the set of *The Skulls* or *Eyes Wide Shut*. What the hell is happening?"

Dr. Swansea hooked an arm through his and then led him deeper into the estate. Beckett was reluctant to go with the man, but his curiosity got the best of him. This was more bizarre than the time when he'd popped acid and rented a canoe in the Philippines.

"In time, Beckett, in time."

A waiter carrying a tray with two drinks walked past, and Dr. Swansea quickly snatched up one of them. Beckett grabbed the other and chugged half of it before turning to face his old friend.

"Is this because of what happened at the Body Farm? Because that was a mistake, an accident."

Dr. Swansea chuckled.

"No, Beckett, it's not because of that."

The foyer opened to an even larger room, one with a circular, elevated stage in the center.

"What is it then? Because I'm getting—hey, is that Sir England? The guy who opened the McEwing Transplant Unit?" Beckett asked, craning his head around to look at a man who walked by. He could've *sworn* it was Sir Francis England in the flesh.

"Who's here is not important—aside from you, of course."

Beckett's brow furrowed, and he took another sip of his scotch.

"Now you're really freaking me out. I gotta tell you, if this is some sort of weird séance, I'm not down with it. And the last old friend I reunited with ended up having a very, well, *interesting* hobby. I'm not sure—"

"You mean Dr. Stransky?" Swansea replied immediately.

Beckett gave him a curious look.

"Y-yeah, that's him. How did you—"

"Just keep on moving, Beckett. It'll all become clear soon."

Dr. Swansea tugged his arm and Beckett was led to the edge of the stage. All around them were people that he recognized; everyone from high ranking members of New York's elite to local celebrities.

Yeah, I need to get out of here. Like, right now.

"Please, Beckett, up here," Dr. Swansea said, gesturing toward the stage. Confused as he was, Beckett originally obliged only to immediately try to get back down again.

"You know what, I don't feel so good, Swansea. I think I'm just gonna go. This isn't... this isn't my *scene.*"

The lights suddenly clicked off and Beckett found himself shrouded in darkness. Worried that he might break an ankle should he leap off the stage in the dark, he elected to stand completely still until the power was restored.

"Dr. Swansea?" There was no reply. "Dr. Swansea?"

"Dr. Beckett Campbell, welcome to DNR," a voice from above belted so loudly that Beckett instinctively ducked.

What the hell?

"Please, we are all friends here," the disembodied voice informed him. "Tell us your story."

Beckett blinked, but the darkness was still all-encompassing.

Friends? Yeah, I don't have too many of those.

"My story? Look, bud, I don't know—"

"Tell us about Winston Trent."

Beckett's blood suddenly ran cold just as the lights clicked on again.

"What are you—"

He stopped when he realized that all the guests had gathered around the stage.

And they were staring at him.

As he scanned their faces, Beckett's vision blurred, as if his head moved more quickly than his eyes.

What the hell was in that drink?

"Tell us about Ron Stransky."

"I'm not telling you shit. I don't know who you people are, but you aren't my friends. I'm outta here."

Beckett went to step off the stage, but the crowd of people suddenly squeezed together, denying him passage. He tried to push them out of the way with his foot, but his movements were sluggish and ineffective.

"Dr. Campbell, we are all here for *you*. Now, tell us your story."

Beckett moved to another spot on the circular stage, but the crowd once again pressed shoulder to shoulder. When he'd entered the castle, Beckett had counted roughly twenty or thirty people inside. Now, however, there seemed to be three or four times that number.

Where are all these people coming from? And what the hell do they want from me?

"Tell us your story," the booming voice ordered again. It was louder now, almost as if it is coming from inside his head.

And then the crowd started joining in; they repeated those same words over and over again, in unison.

"Tell us your story... tell us your story... tell us your story..."

Dizziness threatened to overwhelm Beckett, and he fought the urge to vomit. His head also started to pound, and he gripped his temples in agony. It was as if the PSI in his skull had been ratcheted up to unprecedented levels.

At that moment, Beckett would've done anything to just get off that stage and out of the room. To breathe some fresh air.

Including telling his 'story.'

"All right," he said quietly. When the crowd refused to cease their psychotic chanting, Beckett raised his voice. "All right! *All right!* I'll tell my goddamn story! Just shut the fuck up, already!"

Chapter 57

AT LONG LAST, THE entire room fell silent. To Beckett's surprise, his headache also started to subside.

Then he cleared his throat, bowed his head, and took a deep breath.

Beckett was surprised at how easily the words came.

"It started... it started years ago in Montréal. I was visiting a pathologist friend there and after a lecture, we went out for drinks at a bar. That's when I met her: a beautiful French girl by the name of Pauline DuMaurier, like the cigarettes. She didn't smoke, though, which I thought was a missed opportunity." He'd never told anyone this story before, and yet he was suddenly spilling his guts to a crowd of random people— a group of what looked to be high-powered citizens dressed in suits and chanting like extras from *The Craft*. And yet, once he got started, Beckett found himself unable to stop. "We hit it off well and, after a few drinks, I decided to take her back to my buddy's place. All I had to do was shoot him a look and he nodded, which was just as good as putting a sock on the doorknob."

With his headache completely gone now, Beckett was able to properly observe the crowd. Everyone was staring at him, their eyes locked on Beckett as they hung on his every word.

Don't do this, a small voice in the back of his head pleaded. *Don't do this—this is a mistake.*

But Beckett felt compelled to continue.

"So, I take Pauline back to my friend's place and make her a nightcap. Then we start watching a nature show on TV—there's something about David Attenborough's voice that just never fails to set the mood. Next thing I know, her lips are on mine, and her tongue is desperately trying to enter my mouth."

Beckett paused for effect, and to allow an opportunity for someone to interject or stop him, but nobody said a word. They were barely even breathing, he realized. They were completely, and utterly, captivated.

They're gonna hate you for this, Beckett.

He did his best to suppress a smile.

"Things progressed as naturally on the couch as on the TV, and I eventually worked up the nerve to slip a hand down her pants. I started massaging her, rubbing her at first, and then, unable to contain herself any longer, Pauline thrust her hips upward. So, I did what any medical resident would do in my position: I offered her some release by slipping a finger inside. After a minute or two, she looked up at me with these perfect blue eyes and whispered, *too small.* I thought to myself, all right, I like this girl, and then I slipped a second finger in. I was using both fingers now and her breathing was becoming labored. A minute after that, Pauline looked up at me and again whispered, *too small.* This was new territory for me, but I'm not one to judge. Besides, she was just so damn hot... and tight. Anyway, I shrugged and slid a third finger in. No sooner had I done this did Pauline repeat those two words: *too small.* And now I'm thinking, what the hell? If she needs *four* fingers to get off, then I'm not even gonna touch the damn sides when the pork and beans come out, you know? But I'm a gentleman through and through. After briefly adjusting my arm angle, I tried to accommodate her when her perfect blue eyes went wide, and she roughly grabbed my wrist. Red-faced, Pauline made sure this time to speak as clearly as possible: *doucement, Beckett, doucement.*"

Beckett paused and stared out at the audience. Horrified faces looked back, faces with unhinged jaws and raised eyebrows.

"What? Not a single French person in the audience? Well, I'll help you out, then. Pauline DuMaurier wasn't saying *too small*, as I'd thought she was, but *doucement...* gently."

Chatter immediately erupted, but it wasn't the type of response that Beckett had expected. There were no guffaws, chuckles, giggles, or side-splitting laughter. Still, he didn't let this deter him.

"What? You asked for my story, and there it is. That's what started it all."

Then he raised the middle finger of his right hand to the crowd, the one that ended just after the second knuckle.

"I told you she was tight."

With that, Beckett jumped off the stage, using their confusion to his advantage and slipped between them. He forced his way forward and almost made it to the door without incident. But in the foyer, someone grabbed his arm, and he whipped around.

"Beckett, please, we want to help you," Dr. Swansea pleaded, genuine concern on his face.

"I don't need your fucking help," Beckett shot back as he yanked his arm free.

"Wait—are you having headaches, Beckett?" a desperate Dr. Swansea asked.

Beckett's eyes narrowed, but he continued towards the door without stopping.

"I bet you're having headaches; terrible headaches. I'm also going to go out on a limb here and guess that your fingers tingle all the time. Am I right?"

Beckett gawked.

How does he know? How could he possibly know?

"Yeah, I thought so," Dr. Swansea said with a nod. "And I also know about Winston Trent, and about Wayne Cravat and Ron Stransky."

Beckett finally reached the door and pulled it wide. Then he turned back one final time to look at his old friend.

"And I know that if you come near me again," he shouted as he stepped out into the night, "that I'm going to introduce my fist to your smarmy fucking face."

Chapter 58

EXHAUSTED, CONFUSED, AND CERTAIN that the drink he'd grabbed off the tray had been intended for him—and spiked—Beckett immediately went to bed when he got home. He didn't even bother getting out of his clothes before sliding between the sheets.

As he wriggled to get comfortable, something brushed up against his arm, and Beckett yelped. He instinctively shoved with both feet, and a figure rolled out of bed and fell to the floor.

"Jesus!" a female voice cried. "What the hell was that for?"

Beckett stared down at his girlfriend in disbelief.

"Shit, I'm sorry, Suze," he said quickly, hopping out of bed, and helping her to her feet.

"What the—" Suzan looked up at him. "Beckett! Your face! What the hell happened to your face!"

Beckett brought a hand up to his left eye and winced. Realizing that he was still dressed all in black, he quickly stripped down into his boxers and slid back into bed. Suzan tentatively got in beside him.

"Well, you're not gonna believe this," Beckett began, staring up at the ceiling, "but first, someone threw an envelope at my eye, then I got pepper-sprayed, and, finally, when I went to kiss Grant on the lips, he slapped me. I think the bastard might have scratched me, as well."

"Wh-what? You kissed Grant on the lips?"

Beckett turned to her.

"Yeah, I also got pepper-sprayed."

"But... but you kissed him on the lips? *Why*?"

Beckett looked away.

"It's a long story and I'm afraid it's not all that interesting."

"I beg to differ."

"Suze, I'm exhausted. Can we talk about this in the morning… please?"

He thought that she was going to continue to pester him, after all, this was Suzan Cuthbert, the woman he couldn't lie to and who rarely took no for an answer. But to his surprise, she relented. Instead of asking about his face or his romantic interlude with Grant, however brief, she slowly traced a line down his ribs, only to stop when her fingers reached the gauze.

"New tattoos?"

Beckett stiffened for a moment; he'd completely forgotten about his new ink.

"Yeah…"

"Well, since you won't tell me what they represent, I'm going to assume that they are a tangible reminder of every time we've had sex. And, seeing as we haven't done it for a few days, either you're cheating on me or you went ahead and preemptively added a new line."

Beckett turned to her once more, eyebrows raised.

"I'm not cheating on you," he said bluntly.

"Oh, I know," Suzan replied, slipping a hand into his boxers. "You wouldn't dare do that. Which means that you owe me one."

Beckett was tired, but he wasn't too tired for that.

They made love for longer than usual that night, as Beckett made a conscious decision to take his time. It wasn't just that he wanted to make it memorable—with Yasiv closing in, who knew how much time they had left—but whenever Suzan's mouth parted in ecstasy, he pictured her pretty lips forming a single word: *doucement*.

Yeah, Beckett made sure to be gentle.

Suzan deserved at least that much.

Chapter 59

YASIV STARTLED AWAKE TO the sound of knocking on his car window. His first thought was that it was Dunbar, but then the man spoke, and he knew it wasn't the detective.

"Excuse me, sir, but you can't sleep here." The man knocked again, which was particularly annoying given the fact that Yasiv was staring directly at him and very much awake.

The man appeared to be some sort of security guard and Yasiv quickly pulled out his badge and pressed it against the glass.

"Oh, I'm sorry, sir... sorry to bother you."

Yasiv grumbled something incoherent and then sat up, stretching his back, and wincing at the same time. He didn't remember falling asleep, but evidently, he had, because the sun was now shining and—

Yasiv was suddenly fully awake as his eyes focused on the dashboard.

It was seven thirty-five.

"Shit!" he swore as he hauled himself out of his car.

"Sir, you okay?" the security guard asked.

Yasiv ignored him and then started sprinting towards NYU Medical. Halfway there, he was overcome by a coughing fit and had to stop. After spitting a horrible green and brown wad on the sidewalk, he continued toward the building at a much more moderate pace.

Even though every hallway inside NYU Med looked identical, he had no problem finding the room where he'd dropped off the syringe for testing.

Yasiv had made sure to memorize the route the day prior.

"Hey, Lab Guy!" he shouted as he knocked on the door. "Lab Guy!"

The door opened an inch and a bespectacled eye peered out.

"Can I help you with something?"

"Yeah, it's me; Sergeant Yasiv."

The man started to close the door, but Yasiv jammed his foot in the opening.

"It's me, the one who brought the evidence yesterday? Is your boss here? Did he come in yet?"

The man finally opened the door wide enough for Yasiv to slip inside. Relief washed over him when he saw that there was another man in the room, one who was older, with blond hair, similar glasses, and sporting a pristine lab coat.

"This is the sergeant who brought the specimen in," the tech said as an introduction.

The blond man gave him a once over.

"I'm Dr. Blai—"

"Did you test it? Did you test it for fingerprints?"

The scientist frowned.

"I just signed the supervisory form and was about to put my gloves on. I understand that this is urgent?"

Yasiv nodded excitedly, his eyes darting to the evidence bag still sitting in the fume hood.

"Yeah, it is. How long is this going to take?"

The scientist pulled out a container of black powder and took up residence at the sole chair in front of the hood.

"Depends on the quality of the latent prints. If we have good prints, it won't take long. Five minutes to lift them, and then maybe five more to obtain a satisfactory image using the microscope."

Yasiv's heart was thundering away in his chest now.

This is it... ten minutes, then I'll have you, Beckett. I'll have you dead to rights.

His eyes drifted to the computer monitors on the desk across from the fume hood.

"Is the computer connected to the Internet?"

The two scientists exchanged glances.

"Yes, of course, it is."

Yasiv was unable to suppress a smile.

"Good, then I can upload the print directly into AFIS and look for a match." When neither man moved, Yasiv clapped his hands together. "Come on, let's go, let's go! As I said, this is urgent—real urgent. Now get me those damn prints!"

Chapter 60

BECKETT GRUNTED AND OPENED his eyes. Well, he opened his right eye; his left was swollen shut.

"Fuck me," he groaned. "Suzan, I need a cold compress and an Advil." When there was no reply, he tapped her side of the bed but felt nothing but mattress. "Suzan?"

She wasn't there.

With another groan, Beckett rolled onto his side. He sat on the edge of the mattress for a moment with his elbows on his knees while he waited for the spins to pass.

What the fuck did that asshole Dr. Swansea slip me? He wondered. Whatever it was, it was still wreaking havoc on his system nearly eight hours later.

"Beckett?" Suzan hollered from downstairs. "You up?"

Beckett cleared his throat.

"Yeah, I'm up. Tell me you're making me something cold to drink... my head is killing me."

"I think you should come down here."

There was something about her voice that convinced Beckett to pick up the pace. He found a pair of shorts in the closet and threw them over his boxers, and then made his way downstairs.

"Iced coffee would be fantastic right about now," he said as he entered the kitchen.

When Suzan just stood there, holding an iPad out to him with concern on her face, Beckett frowned.

"What? What is it?"

"You should read this," she said bluntly.

Beckett turned around and started to fiddle with the coffee maker.

"Let me make some coffee first. Need some caffeine to stomach reading about another mass shooting." He was in the process of reaching for the instant coffee when Suzan's words caused him to freeze.

"It's about Reverend Alister Cameron and his wife."

Beckett swallowed hard. Then he took a deep breath and continued to prepare his coffee, trying to act as normal as possible.

"Yeah? What about them?"

"They found their bodies... they found them under two feet of dirt behind their house... the same house that we ate dinner at less than a week ago."

Beckett slowly turned and reached for the iPad. His hand was trembling, but he hoped that Suzan chalked this up to his hangover.

"Looks like someone took them out," Suzan offered.

Beckett barely heard her.

He couldn't believe that their bodies had been found already. Burying them behind the house had been a last-minute decision, and while he knew that eventually they'd be discovered, Beckett had hoped that it would take months.

Not days.

His breathing suddenly became labored.

"Got what they deserved if you ask me."

The more Beckett read, the worse it got. Not only had the local PD, led by a man named Boone Bradley, found the Reverend and his wife's bodies, but there was a passing mention of getting outside help from New York.

They never said *who* helped with the search, but they didn't need to.

Beckett knew that it could only be one man: Sergeant Henry Yasiv.

"Shit," he wheezed.

"No kidding," Suzan replied.

All of a sudden, he recalled Dr. Swansea's words from last night.

We want to help you.

Beckett had told the man to fuck off, had said that he didn't need any help. Sure, a lot of names had been thrown around — Winston Trent, Wayne Cravat, Ron Stransky — but they couldn't *know*. Those DNR or NWA freaks or whatever they called themselves couldn't *know*. Nobody knew the truth... nobody but Beckett.

And yet, if Yasiv had helped discover the bodies, he must have figured out that Beckett had been to South Carolina. And if Beckett had left any shred of evidence behind, any fingerprint or hair or fiber, Yasiv wouldn't be serving a search warrant in the next few hours, but an arrest warrant.

We want to help you.

"Shit," he said again.

Could *Dr. Swansea help him? And if so, how?*

"You okay?"

Beckett put on a fake smile.

"No, no, I'm not — I'm hungover as shit. Listen, Suzan, you think you can do me a favor today?"

Suzan took the iPad back and stared at him blankly.

"Seems like I've been doing a lot of favors for you lately. Including last night."

Beckett pursed his lips.

"I have a feeling that that was mutual. But can you please cover my class today? I've got to go see an old friend about something."

"And I've got—"

Beckett suddenly leaned over the counter and kissed her on the cheek.

"I owe you," he said. "Big time."

Before she could protest further, Beckett bounded up the stairs and was in the shower in under a minute.

"Don't you want your coffee?" she yelled up to him.

"I'll take it to go! Wouldn't be opposed to a little tipple of Jameson in there, either!"

Chapter 61

"WELL, WE'RE IN LUCK; while I couldn't pull a latent off the syringe itself, I've got a pristine thumbprint on some glue that was stuck to the side," the blond scientist said as he held the syringe up to the light. "Should be—"

"Take the picture," Yasiv encouraged. "Just take the picture—I've gotta run it through AFIS right away."

As he watched, the man laid what looked like a thick piece of clear tape over the wad of glue then pulled it off.

"Yeah, this will be perfect. Trevor?"

The younger scientist took the lifted print and laid it on the microscope stage. As he fiddled with the multitude of knobs, the supervisor replaced the syringe back in the evidence bag. He resealed it with red tape, then put his initials across the seam.

Intact... the chain of command is intact.

Yasiv was almost giddy with excitement now, and he had to fight the urge to tell the man peering through the microscope to hurry up.

"Yeah, almost... almost... *there*," he exclaimed.

Yasiv looked at the monitor and smiled. There was a perfect thumbprint in the center of the screen.

"That should be more than—"

The man frowned and looked over at Yasiv, who was already booting up the computer.

"—adequate for comparison purposes."

Yasiv was barely listening. He remotely logged into AFIS, then asked where he could find the image on the hard drive.

"There should be a link on the desktop."

Yasiv double-clicked on the folder marked 'Microscope' and then grimaced. It was full of hundreds of sub-folders.

"Christ, what kind of mess is this? Where is it?"

"Should be under today's date."

Yasiv eventually found the correct folder and opened it. Inside was a single image file, named 'fingerprint'. He dragged and dropped it into AFIS, and then clicked 'Search'. The static fingerprint obtained from the glue remained on the right side of the screen, while the left cycled through tens of thousands of prints that were stored in AFIS.

"How fast is this computer?" Yasiv wondered out loud. "Because this could take some time."

Time I don't have.

"Quad Intel Core i7 processors and thirty-two gigs of—"

The man was interrupted by a ping.

For nearly ten full seconds, Yasiv just stared at the result in utter bewilderment.

The program had found a match. Not only that, but it was a minutiae-based match with a predicted accuracy of greater than ninety-eight percent.

He exhaled sharply.

"I don't... I don't believe it," Yasiv whispered. He double, then triple-checked the results to make sure that he hadn't made a mistake.

He hadn't; everything was exactly as it should be.

"Oh, I've got you now."

Then Sergeant Yasiv inexplicably started to laugh.

Chapter 62

IT WAS AS IF in addition to being the leader of some sort of Gothic Cult, Dr. Swansea was also a telepath. The man was standing in the entranceway to the Body Farm, his hands on his hips when Beckett approached.

And he didn't look pleased.

"Put on some boots, we're going for a walk," Dr. Swansea instructed, forgoing any sort of formalities. Beckett bit his tongue and searched the mudroom for a pair of boots in his size. He found some and slipped them on, then followed Dr. Swansea out the door. They walked for a good ten minutes in silence, passing the location where Taylor had fallen in the mud, before eventually stopping in front of what appeared to be an overturned canoe.

Only then did Dr. Swansea address him.

"What you did yesterday wasn't very bright, Beckett. I had to go to great lengths to clean up the mess you made."

Beckett scratched his head and then winced. The entire left side of his face was still swollen and tender.

"Well, let's just say that I wasn't prepared to be railroaded, to find out that my old friend is actually Neve Campbell from *The Craft*."

Dr. Swansea didn't appear amused.

"Why are you here, Beckett?"

Now it was Beckett's turn to frown. The comment was clearly passive-aggressive in nature, with a heavy emphasis on the latter. It was obvious that Dr. Swansea had seen the article in the Charleston Post and Courier about the good Reverend and his wife.

"Well, the shit has hit the fan, Swansea. I don't know how you found out about Wayne and Winston, or what the fuck

DNR is all about, but I need your help. I'm pretty sure there's an arrest warrant being drawn up for me right now."

Beckett hadn't meant to reveal so much, but the words flowed out of him like loose stool. Maybe it was the drugs that had been slipped into his scotch, or maybe it just felt good to finally get this off his chest.

In the end, it didn't really matter why he'd spoken, only that he had.

"Dr. Ron Stransky," Swansea said, as he stared off into the distance. "That's how we found out about you."

Images of the sickly doctor flashed in Beckett's mind.

Just a drink—one drink. It's a shame to let that good stuff to go to waste. Let me have one drink before it's all over.

"I don't... I don't understand."

Dr. Swansea shrugged.

"You don't have to; not now, anyway."

Beckett chewed the inside of his lip.

"Who are you people? And how can you help me?"

Another shrug.

"In time, we will reveal more about ourselves."

Beckett was too tired for this charade.

"For fuck's sake, this Dead Poet Society routine is getting old *fast*."

Dr. Swansea didn't say anything. He just stood there, hands at his sides, eyes blank and empty.

Beckett sighed. He had no choice but to play the man's strange game.

"Yesterday you said you could help me, and now I need that help."

It pained him to speak these words, seeing as for the better part of his adult life he'd been on his own.

What did Dr. Swansea say when we met the other day? That I was getting soft? Well, maybe I am. Maybe I'm soft and old and in need of some Cialis.

But Beckett knew that he wasn't too old to be a valuable plaything for a sex-deprived inmate.

No, prison just wasn't his bag. So, if this man could really help keep him from landing up behind bars, then he'd swallow more than just his pride.

"Swansea, can you help me?" Beckett repeated.

The man nodded. It was a subtle gesture, one that Beckett barely picked up on. He should have felt relieved, but a tightness started to grow in his chest. Something told him that he'd just entered into an agreement without reading the fine print — or *any* print at all.

And then, without provocation, Dr. Swansea bent down and grabbed the side of the canoe. He flipped it over and Beckett immediately jumped back.

"Jesus!"

Lying on the ground with its arms splayed, was a corpse. It was undoubtedly a man's corpse—a *large* man—but Beckett couldn't make out much more on account of the fact that most of the man's soft tissue had been devoured by insects and wildlife.

"You've made some mistakes, Beckett," Dr. Swansea said calmly. "These can't happen again. You can't leave a body in your shed while you go on vacation."

Beckett choked down some bile.

"Well, I didn't plan on—" His eyes suddenly focused on the corpse again. Despite its advanced state of decomposition, Beckett realized that it looked familiar.

Oh my God, he thought. *That's Wayne Cravat... that's Wayne Cravat's corpse.*

When Beckett finally managed to compose himself, he turned to Dr. Swansea, but the man had already started walking back the way they'd come.

"Dr. Swansea? Ian! *Ian*! Wait up! Don't I get a decoder ring or something? Or in the very least, a poison-tipped umbrella? What the hell kind of club is this, anyway?"

Chapter 63

IT WAS A TOSS-up whether the DA would be at 62nd precinct or at his office. Yasiv guessed the former, and he guessed correctly. Armed with a printout from the lab, he strode briskly past the conference room, deliberately avoiding eye contact with Detective Gabba who was inside.

Even before he pushed his office door fully open, he knew that the district attorney would be sitting behind his desk.

"Sergeant Yasiv, I've been looking for you."

"And I you, DA Trumbo. But, before you say anything, I sent you an email about an hour ago. Yesterday, the bodies of Reverend Alister Cameron and his wife, Holly Cameron, were found buried behind their home in South Carolina. Along with the bodies, part of a syringe was recovered. I had the lab run tests on it and they managed to lift a single latent print off that syringe." Yasiv placed a sheet of paper on the table and slid it across to the DA. "The print was a ninety-eight percent match to none other than Dr. Beckett Campbell."

"I know," DA Trumbo said, not bothering to look at the paper in front of him.

Yasiv's pride and excitement faded a little, but there was no going back now.

"Not only that, but I saw a YouTube video of Dr. Campbell in South Carolina at Reverend Alister Cameron's church."

Once again, the DA seemed nonplussed.

Yasiv had finally obtained the evidence that they needed, a smoking gun, so to speak, but the DA seemed... disinterested at best.

Still, he plodded on.

"Dr. Campbell's DNA was found under Bob Bumacher's fingernails, and we have proof that he was also at Winston Trent's place when the man allegedly committed suicide."

Yasiv realized he was rambling but was unable to stop himself.

"We need to arrest Beckett. And we have to do it today."

The DA just stared at him, blinked once, twice, and then unfolded his arms, revealing a white envelope that had been previously tucked out of sight.

"I know," the DA repeated.

Yasiv's frustration reached a head now.

"What's this?" he snapped as he grabbed the envelope.

"I'm sorry I doubted you, Sergeant Yasiv. You're a man of your word, as am I. In your hands is an arrest warrant for Dr. Beckett Campbell."

Yasiv stared at the plain, white envelope as if it were some sort of ancient relic. Even though the man had spoken plainly and clearly, he still couldn't quite believe it.

"Really?" he asked in a voice just above a whisper.

"Really," DA Mark Trumbo replied boldly. "Now go get this asshole before he kills again."

Chapter 64

BECKETT WAS LOOKING AT his phone—reading a message from Suzan who was asking how he was feeling—when he pulled his Tesla onto his street. He was so distracted and exhausted, that he nearly sideswiped a gray sedan parked several feet from the curb.

"Shit," he swore, dropping his cell phone and gripping the steering wheel with both hands.

There was an unusual number of cars on the street for just past noon on a weekday, but to his relief, a black Lincoln with a busted driver side window wasn't one of them.

Beckett parked in his driveway and sat there for a moment, staring at his house, wondering if Suzan had class or if she was inside.

If she's in there, I'll whip her up one of those omelets she likes. I might add asparagus, even though it goes against everything I stand for.

He got out of the car and started toward his house, only to stop after a half-dozen steps. Beckett turned to inspect the cars again. It wasn't just the sheer number of them that was odd, but it was also the fact that they seemed to be concentrated around his house in particular.

"What the—"

The doors to nearly a half dozen cars suddenly flew open and Beckett found himself the target of an equal number of handguns. And in the lead was a grinning Sergeant Henry Yasiv.

"Dr. Beckett Campbell, put your hands in the air!"

Beckett's heart sank.

I guess you couldn't help me after all, eh, Swansea? He thought as he slowly raised his arms.

Yasiv strode forward, keeping his pistol trained on Beckett's chest. In his free hand, he waved a white envelope dramatically.

"Dr. Beckett Campbell, I have a warrant for your arrest, for the murders of—"

"Put your hands in the air!" several of the other officers shouted.

Beckett looked down at himself.

"My hands *are* in the fucking air!"

"*Hands in the air!*"

Even Sergeant Yasiv appeared confused now. He turned, a strange look on his face.

"Easy now, his hands are—"

"Sergeant Henry Yasiv, put your hands up!"

Chapter 65

Yasiv looked at Detective Gabba as if he'd lost his mind. "What? What the fuck are you talking about? I've got an arrest warrant from the district attorney right here!"

It took him a moment to realize that the guns were no longer trained on Beckett, but on *him*.

"Put your hands up, Yasiv. This is your last warning."

Yasiv didn't put his hands up, but he was smart enough to lay his service pistol on the ground. Then he held the envelope out for all to see.

"You guys are confused… this is an arrest warrant for Dr. Campbell, issued by DA Trumbo himself."

One of the officers roughly tore the envelope from his hand, then wrenched his arms behind his back and cuffed him.

What the fuck is going on? Yasiv wondered, his heart racing in his chest.

The officer who had taken the envelope tore it open and then held it just inches from Yasiv's face.

"What?" Yasiv muttered. "What the hell?"

The envelope was empty.

Shaking his head, he turned to Detective Gabba, who still hadn't lowered his gun, even though Yasiv was now in handcuffs.

"Gabba, what's going on? What's… what's happening here?"

The sound of a car door opening drew Yasiv's gaze. A large man in a bespoke suit and a tie that was just a little too long stepped into the mid-afternoon sun.

It was DA Mark Trumbo.

"Sergeant Henry Yasiv of the 62nd precinct, you're under arrest for the murders of Reverend Alister and Holly Cameron."

Yasiv's jaw dropped.

"No... what? What the fuck are you talking about? This is... what the fuck is this?"

The DA scowled and then started to recite his Miranda rights.

"No," Yasiv pleaded, now shaking his head violently from side to side. "This is a mistake. A fucking mistake. I didn't kill anyone; he did. *He* did."

But despite his words, the startling reality of what had happened suddenly became clear to Yasiv.

They'd screwed him.

He had no idea how or why, but his men and the DA had colluded against him.

They'd screwed him and didn't even have the common courtesy to give him a reach-around.

Or use any lube.

"Yeah, umm, I'm just going to head inside now," a tentative voice said. "If that's okay with you fellas, of course."

Yasiv managed to crane his neck around to see Beckett moving sideways toward his front door.

"I'll get you, Beckett," he hissed.

Beckett made a face and then scampered toward his house.

"I'll get you, Beckett! *I'm going to fucking get you!*"

Chapter 66

DUNBAR WATCHED THE ENTIRE scene play out, a mixture of awe and confusion plastered on his face. He saw Beckett pull into his driveway, and then he saw Yasiv and his men jump out, guns trained.

That's when Yasiv started waving an envelope around, right before cuffs were slapped on him.

From his vantage point down the street, Dunbar could see everything, but couldn't hear what was being said.

He had no idea why Yasiv was being arrested but assumed that it had something to do with Beckett, with pushing too hard, fabricating evidence, perhaps.

Evidence like the plastic bag that Dunbar held in his hands — the one that he'd taken from Yasiv's car when the man had hurried into 62nd precinct with a smile on his face.

He looked at the item in the sealed bag for a moment — some sort of broken syringe — and then raised his eyes to Beckett, who had since started toward his front door. It suddenly swung open and Suzan bounded out. She reached for Beckett and then embraced him tightly.

Yasiv had lost it; Yasiv had gone off the rails trying to convict Dr. Beckett Campbell.

But Beckett hadn't done this. Beckett wasn't a murderer — he couldn't be.

Beckett was a good man, a strange man, at times, but a *good* man.

As he watched the undercover cop cars pull away and Suzan embraced Beckett even tighter, Dunbar slowly peeled back the red tape on the sealed evidence bag.

When Beckett leaned over and kissed Suzan on the forehead, Dunbar reached inside and pulled out the syringe.

And then, when Beckett said something to Suzan and together they walked back into his home, Dunbar opened his driver side door.

Beckett didn't do the things that Yasiv had accused him of. But even if he had, even on the rare, smallest percentage of a chance that the doctor had killed Winston Trent and Bob Bumacher and Reverend Alister Cameron and all the others...

Dunbar shed no tears on their behalf. They were horrible, despicable people who got what they deserved.

Beckett didn't do those things, but even if he did...

Dunbar slowly released his grip on the syringe, then he watched as it fell down the sewer grate and into the water below.

Epilogue

BECKETT USED THE TOOTHPICK that had once skewered a maraschino cherry to stir his Old Fashioned. Then he sighed heavily and took a sip.

He continued this routine every two to three minutes before the seat beside him was finally occupied.

"Rough day?" the man asked as he signaled for the bartender to come over. Beckett waited for him to order a drink before replying.

"One of the worst. You couldn't even imagine."

The man chuckled and when his beverage came—a beer—he drank eagerly.

"I bet I could."

Beckett then turned to face the man, revealing his left eye, which was still swollen and bruised.

"Hey, I know you. Wait... wait..." He circled his own left eye with a finger. "Oh, man, I'm sorry about that. These fucking temp secretaries, they're insane, I tell you."

Beckett frowned.

"Tell me about it."

"So, what happened? What happened with you and... what's his name?" Dr. Gourde asked.

Beckett shrugged and went back to swirling his toothpick.

"Grant... it just didn't work out. You know how these things are."

Beckett took a deep, labored breath.

"I know, tell me about it. I've been having a rough go of it, too. Just the other night, someone broke into my office and then accosted me. Sprayed me in the face with pepper spray. Between you and me, I think it might have been the temp. Didn't tip her or something, I guess—I dunno."

Beckett turned to look at the man, eying him suspiciously.

"Are you serious? Your face looks fine... wait, you better not be hitting on me."

Dr. Gourde smirked.

"And what if I am?" he said, taking another sip of his beer. "There's nothing wrong with that, is there?"

***

"No, not your house," Beckett said as they got into the cab. "Let's go to your office."

Dr. Gourde shrugged.

"All right, if you want. It's closed now, so we'll have the place to ourselves."

Beckett already knew this, because he'd visited it before sidling up to the bar at Dr. Gourde's favorite watering hole.

"But are you sure this isn't gonna give you some sort of PTSD from when you got sprayed?" Gourde said with a laugh.

"Let's just say that the pepper spray was probably the highlight of my day."

Another strange look from Dr. Gourde.

"You're weird, you know that?"

"I've been accused of worse."

Five minutes later, they were in front of Dr. Gourde's private clinic. The man tried to push him up against the doors and kiss him, but Beckett played coy.

"Inside, not here."

"Okay. But the longer you make me wait..."

Dr. Gourde unlocked the front door and then Beckett burst by him, taking the stairs two at a time. When he got to the second-floor landing, he turned back and batted his eyelashes.

"You coming or what?"

Dr. Gourde laughed.

"Not yet."

Jesus, no wonder you're single.

Dr. Gourde opened the door to his private practice next and Beckett once again tried to hurry past. But the doctor was ready for him this time and grabbed his arm.

"No, not so fast," Dr. Gourde said huskily. Before Beckett could wriggle free, the man's lips were on his. Then his tongue was in his mouth, gagging him.

Repulsed, Beckett struggled but couldn't break away. As a last resort, he reached down and grabbed the man by the balls and squeezed.

Hard.

Dr. Gourde finally let go, but he wasn't angry.

He was grinning.

"You're gonna regret that."

"You too!" Beckett giggled. "Quick, in here!"

He ran into the second operating room, which immediately triggered the motion-activated lights. Dr. Gourde followed him in, shielding his eyes.

Unlike Dr. Gourde, however, Beckett wasn't blinded by the incandescent lighting. He'd made a point of staring at the dim bulbs in the hallway, forcing his pupils to constrict. And while Gourde blinked rapidly, Beckett grabbed the syringe he'd laid out on the table behind the man an hour ago and strode forward.

Without hesitating, he drove the needle into the side of the man's neck.

"What the—what the fuck?" Dr. Gourde exclaimed with a gasp.

Beckett wrapped his forearm around the man's throat and leaned in close to his ear.

"If you thought I was weird before, I'm just getting started."

***

Like all the others, the moment that Dr. Gourde awoke, he struggled against his restraints.

"What—what's going on? What's happening?"

His eyes went wide when he saw Beckett dressed in hospital scrubs, complete with a plastic visor that would have made Dr. Karen Nordmeyer envious.

Beckett put a finger to the visor and hushed the man.

"Don't struggle—everyone always struggles. First, they get angry, then sad, then desperate. It's all so damned clichéd."

"I'll kill you; you don't know who I am."

Beckett pointed a gloved finger at Dr. Gourde.

"See? See what I mean? First comes anger."

While Dr. Gourde continued to curse him, Beckett retrieved a bone saw from the table behind him.

When he turned back, Dr. Gourde had transitioned all the way to phase three; he was begging for his life now.

None of this had any effect on Beckett.

"You killed those people; I looked into your records and let's be honest, you're a shitty surgeon. One of the worst I've ever encountered. We're talking getting your medical degree from a Cracker Jack box and your surgical license from a Happy Meal, bad. But, unfortunately, that's not criminal. What is criminal, however, is what you did to Mr. Leacock."

"What are you talking about?" the man gasped.

"I was the one in your office, dickhead. I was the one who sprayed you with pepper spray—I saw your trophies. It was no accident that you botched those surgeries." Beckett brought a hand to the visor, as if to stroke his chin. "Correction, I'm pretty sure that the first few might have been an accident. But then you got a taste for it and after that? After that, you killed on purpose."

"No, no, I didn't—"

Beckett hushed the man again.

"Trust me; been there, done that. I saw the trophies, Dr. Gourde. I *saw* them."

The man started to plead again, which annoyed Beckett. He activated the bone saw, effectively drowning out the whimpering.

When Dr. Gourde looked as if he'd run out of steam, Beckett released the trigger.

"I want you to say it. No, I *need* you to say. Tell me that you killed those people on purpose, and I'll show you mercy."

"I—I—"

Beckett shook his head and then turned the bone saw on again. Only this time, it wasn't for show. He slowly lowered the blade onto the man's bare thigh, letting it sink about an inch deep before pulling it back. Dark red blood bubbled up from the wound and Dr. Gourde let out a chilling shriek.

"Tell me you did it."

The man's eyes rolled back in his head and then his eyelids began to flutter. Thinking that he might lose consciousness, Beckett slapped him across the face.

With tears streaming down his cheeks, Dr. Gourde whispered, "I did it. Just—just stop this. Please, I did it. I killed those people."

And that was enough for Beckett. He raised the saw again, but just before he pulled the trigger, he heard another sound. Only this time, it hadn't come from Dr. Gourde, but from the entrance of the private clinic.

Beckett's heart immediately started to hammer in his chest, and he backed away from the table.

At first, Dr. Gourde appeared perplexed, then he clued in to what was happening.

"Help!" he shouted. "Help! I'm in here! Help me!"

"Shut up," Beckett hissed. "Shut the fuck up."

But Dr. Gourde was just getting started.

"Help me! Help! There's a fucking psycho in here trying to kill me! Help! *Help!*"

Beckett stepped forward, intent on jabbing the man with the saw when the door to the operating room suddenly swung open.

He whipped around and then his jaw dropped.

At that moment, it all made sense. When he'd met Dr. Swansea at the Body Farm the man had said something that didn't register until now.

You can't leave the body in your shed while you go on vacation.

But he *hadn't* left Wayne Cravat's corpse in the shed. He'd left it in the basement.

The bone saw slipped from his hand and clattered to the floor.

"It was you," Beckett whispered as he locked eyes on the person who entered the room. "It was you who moved the body from the basement to the shed... wasn't it?"

END

Author's Note

BECKETT, YOU'RE SO BAD at being... well, bad. But you're hella fun to write.

Maybe he should stick to just helping people, being an ME and an unorthodox professor of forensic pathology. If only his damn fingers would stop tingling and the urges would go away...

The good news? You won't have to wait long to find out. Beckett is back in [Do Not Resuscitate](), which is available now. Just click on the image below to make sure that the second that Beckett's antics are available for human consumption, you'll have it on your Kindle.

As always, you keep reading, and I'll keep writing.

Pat
Montreal, 2019

Printed in Great Britain
by Amazon